FOUR ANGRY MEN

"What's all that yelling?" Joiner said.

"Our amigos across the river," said Slocum. "Coffee?"

Joiner looked across at the angry *rurales*. All four had at last gotten into their trousers and were strapping on their weapons.

"They're pissed off enough to shoot at us," Joiner said.

"They'll have to find their bullets first."

"They'll—"

Joiner started to laugh. "You've done it again," he said. "Yeah. I'll have some coffee."

While they drank their coffee, the *rurales* discovered their weapons were unloaded. The English speaker among them shouted out alone, "Hey, you gringo bastards. You think you got away, huh? You think you played a good joke on us. Well, we'll see about that. We'll see each other again, amigos, and then we'll see who has the last joke."

"You were right, Joiner," Slocum said. "They're pissed off."

DON'T MISS THESE
ALL-ACTION WESTERN SERIES
FROM THE BERKLEY PUBLISHING GROUP

THE GUNSMITH by J. R. Roberts
Clint Adams was a legend among lawmen, outlaws, and ladies.
They called him . . . the Gunsmith.

LONGARM by Tabor Evans
The popular long-running series about U.S. Deputy Marshal
Long—his life, his loves, his fight for justice.

SLOCUM by Jake Logan
Today's longest-running action Western. John Slocum rides
a deadly trail of hot blood and cold steel.

BUSHWHACKERS by B. J. Lanagan
An action-packed series by the creators of Longarm! The
rousing adventures of the most brutal gang of cutthroats ever
assembled—Quantrill's Raiders.

DIAMONDBACK by Guy Brewer
Dex Yancey is Diamondback, a southern gentleman turned
con man when his brother cheats him out of the family fortune. Ladies love him. Gamblers hate him. But nobody pulls
one over on Dex . . .

WILDGUN by Jack Hanson
Will Barlow's continuing search for his daughter, kidnapped
by the Blackfeet Indians who slaughtered the rest of his
family.

JAKE LOGAN

SLOCUM'S
CLOSE CALL

J

JOVE BOOKS, NEW YORK

SLOCUM'S CLOSE CALL

A Jove Book / published by arrangement with
the author

PRINTING HISTORY
Jove edition / April 2000

All rights reserved.
Copyright © 2000 by Penguin Putnam Inc.
This book may not be reproduced in whole or in part,
by mimeograph or any other means, without permission.
For information address: The Berkley Publishing Group,
a division of Penguin Putnam Inc.,
375 Hudson Street, New York, New York 10014.

The Penguin Putnam Inc. World Wide Web site address is
http://www.penguinputnam.com

ISBN: 0-515-12789-2

A JOVE BOOK®
Jove Books are published by The Berkley Publishing Group,
a division of Penguin Putnam Inc.,
375 Hudson Street, New York, New York 10014.
JOVE and the "J" design
are trademarks belonging to Penguin Putnam Inc.

PRINTED IN THE UNITED STATES OF AMERICA

10 9 8 7 6 5 4 3 2 1

1

Charlie Joiner poured himself another drink out of the bottle that stood in front of him on the bar. He'd already had one too many, but then, he didn't have a nursemaid nearby either.

"Señor," said the fat bartender, "do you really mean to go back to Texas in the morning?"

Joiner downed the drink and coughed. He wrinkled his face as if the drink had caused him pain. "Yeah," he said. "Just like I told you, Pee-dro. I'm headed back home. Let them try to stop me. The bastards." He poured another drink.

"But Señor," said Pedro, "if you drink too much, you won't be able to get up in the morning, much less ride."

"I'll tell you what, amigo," said Joiner, "I mean to get drunk tonight, and I still mean to be up with the sun and on the trail back to Texas. I got business to take care of, and it's long past due."

The front door of the cantina opened and a man stepped in. He stood there a moment while the door shut again behind him, and he hitched his gunbelt. He was a gringo with the look of a Texas cowboy. Pedro gave him a broad smile, anticipating some more business, but before he could speak, the smile faded and his eyes opened wide as the stranger pulled a .45 Colt out of his holster and leveled it at Joiner's back. He thumbed back the hammer. "Hold it, hombre," said a voice from the back corner of the room. "Lower that iron."

The stranger hesitated an instant, then swung his gun toward the voice in the corner. There was a flash and a roar from the dark corner. The Texan jerked and winced and involuntarily lowered his revolver. He fired a useless shot into the cantina floor, staggered, and fell onto his face. His right leg twitched once, and then he moved no more. Joiner turned from the bar, his face white. He looked at the body on the floor. Then he looked toward the corner.

"Señor Joiner," said Pedro, "that hombre there on the floor, he was going to shoot you in the backside."

Joiner stepped over to the body and rolled it over with the toe of his boot. "Harman," he said. "Goddamn. He couldn't wait."

The man in the corner stood up and holstered his own Colt. He walked toward the door. As he was about to pass by Joiner, Joiner stopped him. "I owe you a thanks, mister," he said.

"Don't mention it," said the shooter. "I don't like back-shooters."

"At least let me buy you a drink, pard," Joiner said.

"No, thanks. I think I'll ride out of here before the law comes around."

"It was self-defense, Señor," Pedro said. "I am a witness to it. His gun was out first, and he turned on you."

"Just the same," said the other, "I like to steer clear of the law."

"Hey," said Joiner, "what's your name?"

"Slocum."

"Well, Slocum," Joiner said, "I'm Charlie Joiner. Where you headed? Texas?"

"I reckon so," Slocum said.

"I'm headed back that way," said Joiner. "Ride with me."

"I heard you say you're leaving in the morning," said Slocum. "I ain't waiting."

"Then I'll leave now," said Joiner. "I'll ride out with you. What do you say?"

Slocum thought a moment. "How fast can you be ready to ride?" he asked.

"Give me ten minutes," Joiner said. "Hell, make it five."

"All right."

Joiner pulled a coin out of his pocket and slapped it on the bar. He picked up the cork on the bar and poked it back in the neck of his bottle. Then he looked back toward the table where Slocum had been sitting, strode back to it, corked the bottle that was there, and picked it up. Then, a bottle in each hand, he walked back to where Slocum waited and held up both bottles. He grinned. "Okay?" he said.

"Let's go," said Slocum. "Adios, Pedro."

"Adios, amigos," said Pedro. "Gracias."

Slocum and Joiner walked outside. The night air was cool. "It ain't the best time to start a trip," Joiner said.

"No one's making you ride with me," said Slocum.

"Oh, I ain't complaining," said Joiner. "Just making conversation."

"Where's your horse?" Slocum asked.

"In a little corral just down the street there," said Joiner.

"Well," said Slocum, "let's go get him." Slocum walked over to the hitching rail and loosened the reins to the big Appaloosa that was tied there. Then he walked along beside Joiner, leading the horse. Joiner was weaving a bit, but Slocum figured he'd make it all right. He asked himself why he had agreed to let this man ride along with him. Beyond the man's name, Slocum knew nothing about him, except that he was a Texan and someone had wanted to kill him. Hell, he told himself, it was probably a good idea to have company at least to the border. After that, well, he'd see.

They reached the corral and Slocum took the bottles

away from Joiner so that Joiner could saddle his horse. Then he dropped one bottle into his own saddlebag and handed the other back to Joiner, who uncorked it and took a slug before mounting up. Slocum swung up into his own saddle, and the two men rode north together out of the village. If they rode all night, they'd reach the Rio Grande by daylight.

"That man you killed back there, Slocum," said Joiner, taking a slug out of his bottle, "he worked for a man in Texas who don't want me to come back."

"I don't need to know about it," Slocum said.

"Well," said Joiner, "I just thought you might want to know why you killed a man."

"I know why," Slocum said.

"Why?"

"I done told you back yonder," said Slocum. "I don't like backshooters."

"And that's it?"

"That's it," Slocum said.

"You're willing to let it go at that and not know what the hell it was all about?"

"I don't give a damn if he was a U.S. marshal after you for baby-killing," Slocum said. "He shouldn't have been fixing to shoot you in the back."

Joiner took a long drink of whiskey as they bounced along the trail. He pulled the bottle away from his lips with a loud smack. "You're some piece of work," he said.

"I mind my own business," said Slocum. "Mostly."

They rode along a little farther in silence, the only sounds their horses' hooves on the dirt trail and the occasional smacks and gurgles from Joiner's drinking. "You get drunk and fall out of that saddle," Slocum said, "and I'll just leave you lay."

"Hell," said Joiner, "I'm all right."

"Shut up," said Slocum.

"What?"

"Be quiet a minute and listen." Slocum stopped his horse. Joiner stopped his then too. They sat still.

"Someone's coming up behind us," said Joiner.

"Yeah," Slocum said. "Three or four, I'd say."

"What do we do?"

"Get off your horse," said Slocum.

Both men dismounted, and Slocum placed the two horses just beside the road on the right side. Then he had Joiner follow him to the other side of the road and they got down flat on the ground, guns drawn and ready. They waited like that until the riders drew near. In the moonlight, Slocum could make out the *rurales'* uniforms. There were four of them, and they pulled up beside the two riderless horses. Speaking in Spanish, they dismounted and checked the horses. Two of the men walked off to the right side of the road a little further, looking for the men who had left their horses there. The other two stood beside the horses, looking around in the dark.

"Now," Slocum whispered, and he and Joiner jumped up and ran up behind the two *rurales* who stood with the horses. Before the *rurales* knew what had happened, they were staring down the barrels of two Colts. Slocum and Joiner disarmed them. "You *comprende* English?" Slocum whispered.

"*Sí,*" the *rurale* said, his eyes crossed because of the proximity of the barrel of Slocum's Colt to the tip of his nose.

"Call your *compadres* back over here," Slocum said.

The man did so, and when the other two returned, they found themselves covered by two men standing behind their own two men for shields. "Drop your guns," Slocum said. The other two looked curiously at one another.

"They don't talk English, Señor," the man Slocum was using as a shield said.

"Then you tell them what I said," Slocum told him, and the man did. The other two *rurales* dropped their guns. "Now the four of you walk to the other side of the road,"

Slocum told them. They did. "Take off your boots and your pants."

When that last command was translated, all four *rurales* began talking at once in Spanish. Slocum didn't understand it, but he could tell it was indignant protestation. He fired a round from his Colt into the ground in front of the *rurales*, and they stopped talking at once, sat down, and pulled off their boots. Then they stood again to shed their trousers. Slocum told the one who could understand him to put the boots and trousers on their horses.

"Joiner," he said, "gather up their guns. I'll take the horses, and we'll lead them off a ways."

"Señor," said the English speaker, "you don't mean to leave us here like this."

"Amigo," said Slocum, "you all can start walking behind us anytime you feel like it. We'll leave your horses and britches and boots and guns all on this side of the Rio Grande. By the time you get to them, though, we'll be long gone on the other side."

"Please, Señor—"

"Let's go," Slocum said.

They rode at a trot toward the river, and Joiner suddenly burst into laughter. When he finally quieted down some, Slocum said, "What's so damn funny?"

"What's funny?" Joiner said. "Why, what you done to them *rurales*, of course. What did you think?"

"You wouldn't think it was funny if I'd done it to you," Slocum said.

"Well, I—"

"I didn't do it to be funny," Slocum said. "Done it to slow them down."

A little later, Slocum slowed their pace. "They'll never catch us now," he said. "No need to wear out our horses."

Joiner pulled the bottle out of his saddlebag again, uncorked it, and took a slug of whiskey as they rode along. In another mile, he threw the empty bottle to the side of the road. Two miles on farther down the road, he fell off his horse. Slocum stopped and looked down. Joiner didn't move. "Damn," said Slocum. He thought about the threat he had made to Joiner earlier, and then he thought about the four *rurales* who would almost certainly be very angry by this time. They would also most likely arrive at this spot before Joiner came out of his stupor.

Slocum dismounted, dragged Joiner up, and shoved him across his saddle. Then, still holding the reins of the four *rurales'* horses, he took also the reins of Joiner's horse to lead. He rode along at an easy pace the rest of the way to the Rio Grande. There he turned loose the four captive horses, leaving guns, boots, and trousers as well. Riding well into the river, he pulled Joiner's horse up beside him, reached over, and shoved Joiner off into the cold water. Joiner hit with a splash, roared, went under, then came back up spluttering and spitting. When he at last recovered from the shock, he stood up. The water was just below his waist.

"Where the hell am I?" he said.

"In the Rio Grande," Slocum said, "Mount up and let's get across and make a camp."

"Goddamn," Joiner said. "What the hell happened?"

"You passed out," Slocum said. "Come on. We'll build a fire to dry you out."

Joiner swished his way through the water to the side of his horse and climbed into the saddle with a groan. "Oh, my head," he said.

"If you can't handle it," Slocum said, "you shouldn't drink so much."

"I can handle it, all right," Joiner said.

"That why you fell in the river?"

They rode out on the other side, and Slocum selected a spot for a camp within easy view of the river. He gathered up some sticks and built a fire, then unsaddled the horses. Joiner stripped and laid out his wet clothes near the fire. Laying out his blanket roll, he found a clean pair of long underwear to put on. Then he stretched out on his blanket to sleep. Slocum spread his own blanket and took his bottle out of his saddlebags. He pulled off his boots, then took off his gunbelt, placing it within easy reach, and leaned back against his saddle. He took a long drink of whiskey. It was good.

Slocum was boiling some coffee over the fire in the morning when he saw the four *rurales* arrive across the river. At first they were too busy catching their horses and finding their trousers to notice anything else. Then one of them saw the campfire and recognized Slocum. With one leg in his trousers, the *rurale* shouted angrily. *"Bastardos!"* He hopped around, trying to get his other leg in. *"Bastardos gringos."*

The other three looked then and saw Slocum in his camp. "Goddamn Americanos," shouted one.

Joiner raised his head. "What the hell?" he said.

"How you doing this morning?" Slocum asked.

"What's all that yelling?" Joiner said.

"Our amigos across the river," said Slocum. "Coffee?"

Joiner looked across at the angry *rurales*. All four had at last gotten into their trousers and were strapping on their weapons. "What did you stop here for?" Joiner asked.

"They can't come over here after us," said Slocum.

"They're pissed off enough to shoot at us," Joiner said.

"They'll have to find their bullets first," said Slocum.

"They'll—"

Joiner started to laugh. "You've done it again," he said. "You son of a bitch." He got up and found dry trousers from his roll and pulled them on. "Yeah," he said. "Yeah, I'll have some coffee."

While they drank their coffee, the *rurales* took aim with their weapons, and soon discovered that they were unloaded. Another string of shouted Spanish oaths followed. Then the English speaker among them shouted out alone. "Hey, you gringo bastards," he called out. "You think you got away, huh? You think you played a good joke on us. Well, we'll see about that. We'll see each other again, amigos, and then we'll see who has the last joke."

"You were right, Joiner," Slocum said. "They're pissed off."

The two men finished their coffee, put out the fire, and saddled and packed their horses. The four *rurales* were still shouting and shaking their fists from the other side of the river when Slocum and Joiner mounted up to ride on. Slocum waved at them. "So long, amigos," Joiner shouted. "It's been a whole lot of fun."

In a short while they had ridden over a rise and the Rio Grande was no longer in sight, nor, of course, were the *rurales*. Now and then Joiner still chuckled. They rode a while longer without talking, and then Joiner broke the silence. "Slocum," he said, "can I tell you why that bastard back there in the cantina was fixing to backshoot me?"

"If it's just tormenting you to tell me," Slocum said, "go on."

"I had me a spread up here a couple of years back," Joiner said. "I was doing all right. Then folks started losing cattle, and a man named Harman accused me of the rustling. He brought a band of vigilantes out to my place, and they found some of my neighbors' cows there. It was the first I knowed about it. Harman put them there, I'm sure. Anyhow, they wouldn't listen to me. They was ready to string me up. I put up a fight and barely got out of there with my hide. I carried a couple of bullets away with me too.

"Well, I scooted down across the border to nurse my wounds and hide out, but I done more than that. When I was able, I snooped around some, and I found me some proof that Harman was the one been selling stolen cattle in Mexico. I got statements from the men he sold them to, and I mean to go back home and prove it on him and get my ranch back. I think he found out that I had got it and was coming back, and that's why he sent that gunnie after me."

"So that's what you meant back there," said Slocum. "I

thought I heard you calling that one I shot Harman, but what you meant was that he had been sent by Harman."

"Right," said Joiner.

"How'd he find out what you know?" Slocum asked.

"Hell," said Joiner, "he's still in the business. Some of his trips down this way, someone told him I'd snooping around."

"Yeah," said Slocum. "That makes sense. So why'd you want to tell me all this?"

"Well," Joiner said, "I didn't want you to think that you'd maybe killed a man who had a good reason to be gunning for me."

"I told you," said Slocum.

"I know," Joiner said. "You don't like a backshooter. I still wanted you to know. Besides, I'd like for you to go back with me. I want you to help me get Harman put away and help me get my ranch back."

2

"I ain't interested," Slocum said.

"Aw, come on, pard," Joiner said. "I can't pay you nothing right now, but when I get my ranch back, I'll have plenty. I'll pay you good then. You got my word on it. Come on. What do you say?"

"I said it already," Slocum responded. "I ain't interested. I don't like fighting, even for myself. I sure don't hanker to get involved in someone else's fights. Besides, I'm headed west."

"You got any money?" Joiner asked.

"Nope," said Slocum. "I left the last of it back in that Mexican cantina."

"Well, there you go," Joiner said. "You need a job."

"What you're offering don't sound like much of a job to me, Chuckie boy. You're as broke as me, and if you get yourself killed somewhere along the way, I won't ever get paid. Especially if I was to get killed along with you."

"Slocum," said Joiner, and then he hesitated. "Say," he continued, "you got a first name?"

"It's John."

"All right, John," Joiner went on, "listen to me. I know that you and me together can take them. And with these documents I'm carrying, we'll have the law on our side too."

"Forget it," Slocum said. "Hunt yourself another gun-hand. They're a dime a dozen."

Joiner frowned, and the two rode on a ways in silence. Up ahead a small grove of trees stood beside the road in a tangle of thicket. Suddenly a shot rang out, and Slocum felt a sharp, burning pain in his left shoulder. He yelled in surprise and pain, and in spite of himself, he slipped from the saddle and fell hard onto the road. He heard a pounding of hooves and another shot, then more, and then he saw nothing but a black swirl. He was aware of nothing.

Slocum's consciousness slowly came back to him, but he saw the room around him in a swirl. He tried to blink his vision back straight, but it was no use. He closed his eyes tight and tried to remember something, anything. Then it came back to him. He'd been riding along the road with Joiner and . . . What? There had been the sound of a shot and . . . Someone had shot him. He recalled the setting, the trees up ahead. It must have been a rifle shot, and it must have come from the trees. But where the hell was he, and what about Joiner?

He felt a soft touch on his forehead, and he opened his eyes again. He found himself looking up into a vision of loveliness, a young blonde with deep blue eyes and full, luscious lips. She was leaning over him with a look of concern on her face, and the way she was leaning, with the top two buttons of her shirt undone, he had yet another lovely vision, this one of a most inviting cleavage between two marvelous, firm-looking breasts.

"Hello," he said.

"You're awake," she replied. "Oh, good. We were awfully worried about you."

Her voice was as sweet as the rest of her. Slocum felt a strong desire to reach up and pull her down to him, but he didn't know her, didn't know where he was, and she had said "we."

"You and who else?" he asked her.

"Why, Charlie, of course," she said. "Who did you think?"

"I had no idea," he said. "Who are you."

"I'm Myrtle," she said. "Myrtle Bingham. You're in my house. I was Charlie's neighbor—before he lost his ranch."

"Where is—Charlie?" Slocum asked.

"I don't know," she said. "He said he was going out to scout around."

"Are you and Charlie—"

"Hush now," Myrtle said. "You're just full of questions, aren't you. Right now I'm going to get you something to eat. You've been out for quite a spell. You must be hungry, and you need food to help get your strength back."

He hadn't noticed with his eyes full of Myrtle, but as soon as she mentioned food, he felt the gnawing in his stomach. He wondered then just how long he had been out. How much blood he had lost. How long it had taken Joiner to get him there. As Myrtle walked out of the room he watched her ass, jeans stretched tight over it, swing itself through the door. Well, if he was going to eat, he'd need to sit up. He raised his head and moved his elbow to help himself up, and a pain shot through his body. He fell back. "Damn," he said.

He took a deep breath, set his jaw, and tried again. It hurt, but this time he managed to pull himself up to a sitting position and lean back against the headboard of the bed. He leaned his head back and sucked in deep breaths waiting for the pain to subside. He heard the sound of a horse approaching, and in another moment, a door opening and closing again. Then he heard footsteps in the other room. He looked around the room for his gunbelt, but he didn't see it anywhere. Then he heard a voice. "Myrtle. Where are you?"

He relaxed a little then. It sounded like Joiner, even in

its attempt at a harsh whisper. Then he heard Myrtle say, "It's all right, Charlie. He's awake."

In another moment the door opened to the room he was in and Joiner stepped through. "Slocum," he said. "I'm sure glad to see you awake. For a while there, I wasn't sure you ever would be." Then Myrtle edged her way past Joiner and walked over to the bed carrying a tray. She put the tray on the bedside table and spooned up some beef stew for Slocum. He slurped it out of the spoon.

"I'm awake, all right," he said to Joiner. "I can tell by how bad it hurts."

Myrtle thrust another spoonful at his mouth, and he took it in.

"That's mighty good, Miss Bingham," he said.

"Call me Myrtle," she said, and stuck another spoonful up to his lips.

"Chuckie boy," Slocum said, "what the hell happened back there?" He opened his mouth for the stew, and Myrtle shoved it in.

"Chuckie boy?" she said.

Joiner ignored her and started to answer Slocum's question. "We was just riding down the trail," he said. "We was coming up on a grove of trees. I should have known better, 'specially since that one backshooter came at me in the cantina. I should have expected another ambush like that. Anyhow, one of Harman's bastards shot you from the trees."

"I kind of figured that much," Slocum said. "Go on."

Myrtle spooned him some more stew, as Joiner continued his tale.

"Well," he said, "I threw myself off my horse and rolled over to the side of the road just as he fired again. He must have thought he'd hit me too. I laid there real still-like for—I don't know how long—but finally he come out of the woods. He come walking toward us real slow, like he wasn't sure if we was dead or not, and since I was the closest to him, when he got within maybe twenty feet or so, he started to raise up that rifle again. Well, hell, it wasn't the surest revolver shot you could want, but I didn't have much choice. I raised up my Colt real quick-like and drilled the bastard. It was a lucky shot, I guess. Anyhow, he fell dead. I loaded you up and got right over here as fast as I could. It's the only safe place I could think of."

"I reckon we're even now," Slocum said.

"Not exactly," said Joiner. "You wouldn't have took that slug if you hadn't been riding along with me."

"I still say we're even," Slocum said.

"Okay," said Joiner. "Have it your way. Anyhow, you'll likely be on your feet in another day or two. Eating Myrtle's good cooking will get you your strength back in a hurry. Then you can be on your way west. I'm sorry I got you shot up, friend. Good luck in your travels."

"I ain't going anywhere real soon," said Slocum. "We got a ranch to get our hands on."

"We?" Joiner said.

"You heard me," said Slocum.

"You said you didn't want no part of anyone else's fight," said Joiner.

"The son of a bitch had me shot, didn't he?" Slocum said. "That makes it my fight."

"Damn, Slocum," Joiner said. "That almost makes me glad you got shot." Two long steps took him to the bedside. He stuck his right hand out over Myrtle's shoulder. Slocum reached up and gripped it with his own. "I'm sure glad to have you with me, John," Joiner said. "Sure glad."

As Joiner released his grip, Slocum winced. The pain was not from Joiner's grip. It had come from the movement of Slocum's arm. He wondered how long it would take to really mend. Myrtle spoon-fed him again, and Joiner paced the room with excitement. "Bastards better watch out now," Joiner said. "Charlie Joiner and John Slocum are coming."

"Charlie Joiner and John Slocum better watch out," Slocum said. "How many men has this Harman got?"

"Oh, well," Joiner said, "I ain't for sure. Let's see.

There's about, I'd say, a dozen cowhands on the ranch."

"Cowhands or gunfighters?" Slocum asked.

"I'd say they was likely both," said Joiner. "They're rustlers. That's for sure. That means they got to be able to handle cows, but they also got to be ready for trouble."

"That makes sense," Slocum said. "About a dozen, huh?"

"And six or eight hardcases in town at the saloon," Joiner said.

"What saloon?" Slocum said. "What're you talking about?"

"I went out scouting around while you were out," Joiner said. "It seems that Harman took the profits from my ranch, and likely from his rustling, and went and bought the Hi De Ho Saloon in Rat's Nest. He keeps a bunch of bouncers and bodyguards in there with him."

"That makes around twenty," Slocum said. "What else have you forgot to tell me about?"

"That's all, John," said Joiner.

"It's not all," Myrtle said, shoving a spoonful of stew into Slocum's mouth. "With all his money, everyone in Rat's Nest depends on Harman's goodwill, one way or another. If it comes to a showdown, you don't know which way they'll turn."

"What about the law?" Slocum asked.

"We have a county sheriff," Myrtle said. "He means well, but there doesn't seem to be anything he can do. He says he's got no proof of any wrongdoing on Harman's part."

"I've got it now," Joiner said.

"Then the trick is to get it to him without being stopped somewhere along the way," said Slocum. "Has he got deputies?"

"Two of them," said Myrtle. "Eddie Cobb's all right. I'm not sure about Joe Short. He could go either way. Like the town folks."

"Tell me something else," Slocum said. "Has Harman got a legal claim to your ranch?"

"I don't know," Joiner said. "I had to get out of here fast, like I told you before. The next thing I heard, he'd moved out there and taken over."

"He's got it," said Myrtle. "Charlie's right. When he left, Harman just took posession. No one seemed to care. Then when the taxes came due, the place was put on the sheriff's auction, and Harman bought it—for next to nothing. No one dared to bid against him."

"So even if we prove him a rustler," said Slocum, "He'll still own your ranch."

"It won't do him any good in prison," Joiner said, "or dead."

"Can you get your evidence to Sheriff—what's his name?" Slocum said.

"Bud Coleman," Myrtle said.

"Can you get to Coleman with that evidence without anyone seeing you along the way?" Slocum asked Joiner.

"I don't know," Joiner said. "I think so. I could go to his house after dark."

"Well, don't try it just yet," Slocum said. "I don't know what the hell I'd do laid up here like this if you went and got yourself killed."

Myrtle spooned the rest of the stew into Slocum's mouth and put the spoon and bowl back onto the tray. "That's enough talking for the day," she said. "Let's get out of here and let him rest."

"Hold on," Slocum said. "I been asleep ever since I took that bullet. Right now I could really use a cup of coffee."

"All right," Myrtle said. "I'll get it." She took the tray and left the room.

"That's quite a woman you got there, Chuckie," said Slocum.

"What?" said Joiner. "Oh. You mean Myrtle? Me and Myrtle? No. You got it wrong, pard. Oh, she's a good friend. Has been for years now, but that's all. There ain't nothing more than that between us. Just good friends."

"Oh, yeah?" Slocum said. He tried not to show too much

delight in that good news. "How could you be good friends with someone like that and not—well, you know?"

"I got a girl in town," Joiner said. "Her and Myrtle is good friends. I couldn't take you there 'cause someone would have seen us go into town. In fact, I ain't seen her yet since we been back up here, and I'm dying to."

"You try going into town," said Slocum, "you might be just plain dying."

"I know that," said Joiner, "but I sure am craving to see her. Her name's Julia. Julia Foster. When we get my ranch back, I aim to marry up with her."

"Well, Chuckie," said Slocum, "I hope it won't be long. I just wish I wasn't laid up like this."

"Ah, you won't be for much longer, John," said Joiner. "You'll be as good as new in a few days. Then we'll go after them."

"Chuckie," Slocum said, the tone of his voice indicating a change of subject, "how well do you know this Coleman?"

"The sheriff?" said Joiner. "I've known him for a few years. We never was drinking buddies or nothing like that. But I trust him. He's honest. I'm sure of it."

"You'd better be sure of it," said Slocum. "If you take that evidence of yours to him, and he chooses not to do anything with it or to give it up to Harman, then you're back where you started. And this time you can't go running back to Mexico. Those four *rurales* will be waiting for you."

"I trust him," said Joiner.

"All right," Slocum said, "but let's wait a day or so. Let's wait till I can get up and around. Then I'll go see Coleman."

"You?" Joiner said. "Why you?"

" 'Cause only one of Harman's men has seen me," Slocum said, "and you killed him. No one'll know me, and I won't have any problems getting into town. That's why. I won't carry your papers with me. I'll just talk to Coleman and find out what he'll do if we present the papers to him. We'll figure out our next move after that. In the meantime, I think you ought to stay close around here. They know you're back by now. Harman's sent two men out to get you, and neither one of them got back to him. He'll have men looking for you all over the place."

"I ought to be doing something," Joiner said.

"Yeah," Slocum said. "So should I, but that gunshot I took is going to slow us both up for a while. Live with it."

Myrtle came back in the room with three cups of coffee on her tray. Joiner stepped aside so she could get to the bedside table. She put the tray down and took a cup off it, holding it out to Slocum. "Can you handle it?" she asked.

"Yes," he said, taking the cup. "Thanks."

He slurped the hot coffee, then sighed. "Ah," he said, "that's good."

Myrtle handed a cup to Joiner, then took one for herself. "You want our company," she asked, "or would you rather we get out of here and leave you alone?"

"I'm wide awake," Slocum said. "I'd just as soon have company, if you don't mind. That is, unless you have something else to do."

"There's always something else to do around a place like this," Myrtle said, "but it can wait."

"I, uh, I think I'd better go tend to our horses," said Joiner. He took a final sip of coffee, put the cup down, and left the room. Slocum looked up into Myrtle's deep blue eyes. She sipped coffee.

"I owe you a lot, lady," he said.

"Forget it," she replied.

"I won't. You can be sure of that."

"Why are you looking at me like that? What are you thinking?"

"I ain't at all sure that I ought to tell you what I'm thinking."

She leaned in closer to him. "Tell me," she said.

"All right. I was thinking that if my arm and shoulder

would stand it, I'd be hard-pressed to keep myself from throwing an arm around you and pulling you down close to me, and—"

She leaned even closer and stopped his mouth with a kiss, a warm, luscious, long kiss, and then parted her lips and slid her tongue in between his lips. He opened his mouth to allow her in, and her tongue probed and explored the inside of his mouth. At last she pulled away.

"Lady," said Slocum, "I hope you ain't starting something that I can't finish."

"You just lie still and relax," she said. "I'll finish it."

3

She pressed her lips against his again, and again she probed his mouth with her tongue. Slocum felt a rising between his legs, and for the first time since he had regained consciousness, he realized that he was stark naked under the sheet. He wished that he had all his normal strength, but then, Myrtle had volunteered for this, so he would let her perform. She pulled away from his lips and lowered her head to his chest, where her tongue flicked his nipples. At the same time, her left hand roamed over his chest, then lower onto his stomach, and at last went between his legs to stroke his heavy balls. Slocum moaned quietly.

Myrtle shoved the sheet down out of her way, and her lips and tongue crawled their way down his belly, lower and lower, until she uncovered his now-hard and throbbing rod. She gripped the shaft tight and felt it pulse in her palm. Then with one hand she continued to stroke his balls, while with the other she slowly pumped the stout cock. Slocum meant to lie still and enjoy it, but in spite of himself, he started to thrust with his hips, slowly thrusting his cock into her hand.

Her face moved closer to the scene of the action. She leaned over his body, and shot her tongue out to give a quick lick to the head of his prick. Slocum's entire body gave a twitch at the suddenness of the thrill. She licked again, and again, as if she were slurping at a piece of hard candy. "Umm," she moaned with pleasure. "This is nice." Her lips parted then and eagerly, like a cat pouncing on a mouse, clamped around the head of his cock. She held it there, lapping her tongue around it, driving him wild. He wanted to thrust deep into her mouth, down her throat, but she still held the shaft tight in her hand.

She moved her head again and licked at his balls. Then she backed away, stood up, and took hold of the sheet. She flung it clear to the foot of the bed, revealing all of Slocum's naked body. "Real nice," she said. She walked to the foot of the bed and crawled in between his legs, stroking the inside of his thighs all the way until both hands wrapped around first his balls, then his shaft. Then she suddenly pounced on his cock with her open lips, taking almost the entire length in at once. She held it there a moment, savoring its taste and its feel, thrilling each time it throbbed and tried to jump inside her mouth. Then she pulled back until all she held between her lips was the head. And she plunged downward again.

Slocum picked up her rhythm, and each time she dived down on his rod, he thrust upward with his hips, driving it faster and harder into her luscious mouth. He was fucking her face, and it was great. She was obviously enjoying it too. It felt good, and he wanted it to last forever, but it had been too long, and he was too horny. He felt the surge build up, and he knew that he couldn't hold it back much longer. Suddenly he didn't even want to hold it back any longer. He thrust harder, faster, and he felt it burst forth, gushing into her eager mouth. She slurped harder, swallowing each burst he gave her. At last he relaxed. She held his cock in her mouth a little longer, feeling it begin to soften. Finally, she backed off. She held it tight by the shaft again, and she squeezed and pulled, milking a last drop and licking it off the head of his cock.

Slocum heaved a great sigh. "Lady," he said, "that was

truly wonderful, but I do feel just a bit guilty at not having pleasured you."

"Hush," she said, backing out of the bed. She stood up and pulled the sheet back over his body, then walked back to the chair that stood beside the head of the bed. She sat down and leaned over him again, planting her lips on his for a tender kiss. "I enjoyed myself," she said, "and there'll be other times."

"I'm glad to hear that," he said. "But I can't help being curious. You don't even know me. Not really. Ole Chuck brought me in here more dead than alive, all stove up and—"

"And I took care of your wounds," she said, interrupting him. "I had to undress you, and wash you—all over. I got to know you pretty well. I liked what I saw—and handled."

"Well," Slocum said, "I'm sure glad you did."

Before the day was over, Slocum was getting up and back down without assistance. When Myrtle had prepared the next meal of the day, he said that he could go to the table with the other two, but she insisted that he stay in bed, and served him there. The next morning, however, he was up and dressed early. When Myrtle came in to bring him his first cup of coffee, she stopped, astonished.

"Just what the hell do you think you're doing?" she said.

"Just what it looks like," he replied. "I've got to start moving around sometime."

"But not too soon," she said.

"Damn it, I'm all right," Slocum insisted. "The only thing I can't quite manage yet is to pull on my boots. I tried it, and it just hurt too much. So if it's okay with you, I'll roam around the house without them for now. And that coffee sure smells good."

"Oh, here," she said, thrusting the cup at him. He took it and took a tentative sip.

"Ah," he said. "It's as good as I thought."

"What do you mean?" she asked him.

"Well, yesterday when you brought me coffee, I wanted it so bad, any old kind of coffee would have tasted good. I thought it was good then. Now I know it is. Thanks."

"You're welcome," she said. She was still huffy. "Breakfast will be ready soon. Since you're feeling so chipper, you can come to the table—in your bare feet."

Slocum followed her out of the room. He found Joiner sitting at the table with a cup of coffee in front of him. "Morning, Chuckie boy," he said.

"Good morning, John," Joiner said. "Hot damn. This is a surprise. I didn't expect to see you up and around for a few days yet. Damn but you're one tough son of a bitch."

Slocum put his cup on the table and sat down across from Joiner. "I manage," he said.

"Something happen in there last night to help you regain your strength?" Joiner said with a grin and a wink.

"That ain't none of your business, Chuckie," Slocum answered. "What have you been up to?"

"Oh, when I left you," Joiner said, "I rode up on the hill overlooking my ranch. I stayed there a while hoping to see something, but things was pretty quiet. Then I rode most of the way to town, but I seen Harman's men watching every damn road. They sure do know I'm back, and they're looking for me. I couldn't find a way into town for nothing, so after a while I just come on back here."

"That was a damn fool thing for you to try," Slocum said. "You might have got your fool self killed."

"That's what I figured out," Joiner said. "I sure am dying to see Julia, though. Likely she's heard that I'm back by now. She'll be wondering why I ain't got in touch with her."

Myrtle stepped out of the kitchen with a coffeepot just then and refilled their cups. "I can go see her for you," Myrtle said. "I need to go to town for supplies anyhow. If you'll hitch up the wagon for me, I'll take care of those two chores right after breakfast."

"I can sure handle that," Joiner said.

"But you have to promise me that you'll stay put till I get back," Myrtle said. "I don't want you going off and leaving John here by himself."

"I'll stick like glue," Joiner said.

She served them a fine breakfast of bacon, eggs, fried potatoes, biscuits, and gravy, and after he'd had another cup of coffee, Joiner went outside to get the wagon ready for Myrtle. In the meantime, she got herself ready to go. Joiner came back inside. "The wagon's ready," he said.

She put her hat on her head. "I'll be a couple of hours," she said. "You know where everything is. And Charlie, you take good care of him."

"I will," Joiner said. "I promise."

She was about to go out the door when Slocum stopped her with a word. "Myrtle," he said. She stopped and turned back to face him. "You be careful too," he said. "If Harman and them know that you and Chuckie are friends, you could be in danger—or they might follow you back here. Watch yourself."

"Don't worry," she said. "I can take care of myself."

She went outside and shut the door, and in another moment Slocum could hear the sound of the wagon being driven away. Suddenly he missed the sight of her. He thought about the way her jeans were stretched tight over her lovely rear end, and then he thought ironically of what he had done with her, or what she had done to him, and the sad fact that he had never even seen her bare ass. He wanted to see all of her, and he wanted to make real love to her. He waited a little while, and then he said, "Chuck, go saddle your horse and follow her. Keep out of sight, but make sure nothing happens to her."

"But she said—"

"I know what she said," Slocum snapped. "Follow her. Unless she gets herself in some kind of trouble, she'll never know."

Joiner strapped on his Colt, put on his hat, and left the house. Shortly, Slocum heard him ride off. He stood up with a moan and went into the kitchen for some more coffee. It sure would be nice, he thought, to have a drink of good whiskey and smoke a good cigar. He found the coffeepot and poured the last of its contents into his cup. Back at the table, he sat down again with a moan. Myrtle was right. Maybe he was pushing it too hard and fast. He drank the coffee and walked back into the bedroom, where he stretched himself out on the bed. He was still mighty sore.

Sore and tired, but not sleepy. He lay there wide awake thinking about his situation. He had let himself in on the troubles of Chuck Joiner. Of course, he had done it on purpose because some son of a bitch had shot him from ambush, and he meant to be even for that. Still, here he was, with one other man, fixing to face up to maybe twenty gunhands, maybe more. He had to admit to himself that it was crazy. If he had any brains, he told himself, he'd lay around a couple more days and get healed up pretty good, then ride out. But then, he thought, he never did have any brains.

Joiner thought that the sheriff could be trusted, and Myrtle seemed to agree with that. He sure hoped that they were right, but he hadn't met many sheriffs in his time that he would trust. He meant to go carefully moving in that direction. Other than the possible help of the sheriff and his two deputies, there was no one else. Just two girls. The odds were terrible. But he was mad, and he had opened his big mouth and made a promise. He guessed that he was in this all the way to the finish.

And then there was Myrtle. He sure wasn't done with her. There was a lot more of her he wanted to see, especially that ass, and there was a lot more he wanted to do with her. Hell, he guessed that that was worth taking a chance on getting killed over. He'd taken bigger risks in his day for a hell of a lot less. She was sure one lovely lady. He wondered why she was still unbranded, a beautiful woman like that. He wondered why, but he was sure glad that she was still a maverick.

• • •

He heard the pounding of hooves outside and sat up quickly, causing a pain to shoot through his body. Then he realized that he had, after all, gone back to sleep. He got up off the bed and found his Colt, then went into the main room to look out a front window. He relaxed. It was Joiner. He put the Colt back in the bedroom and waited for Joiner to come in. It took a few minutes, and Slocum figured that Joiner was putting his horse away. At last, Joiner came through the door.

"What's up?" Slocum said.

"Everything's all right," Joiner said. "I followed her to town and lurked around till she headed back out. Then I tailed her again. When we was close enough, I got out around her and hurried on back so she wouldn't know. Just like you said. She'll be driving up shortly, and when she does, I'll just go out there and act like I've been waiting here with you all the time."

"Good," Slocum said. He rubbed his eyes. "Why don't you see if you can boil up some more coffee?"

"I can do that," Joiner said, and he headed for the kitchen.

By the time the coffee was ready, and Joiner had poured a couple of cups full, they heard the wagon pull up out front. Joiner put down his cup and went outside. After a few trips back and forth, he and Myrtle had unloaded all the supplies. Joiner excused himself to go back out and take care of the wagon and team. Myrtle busied herself putting things away in the kitchen. Slocum followed her in there.

"Any problems?" he said.

"No," she said. "I did see some of Harman's men, but they didn't seem to pay much attention to me. In town I did my shopping and then went by to see Julia. I told her Charlie's out here, and she got all excited. She'll be coming out later. I told her to be careful and not let anyone follow her out here. Ed Cobb saw me as I was leaving Julia's house. He didn't seem to think anything about it. Everyone knows that me and Julia's been friends for years."

"Okay," Slocum said. "I'm glad you're back."

She had just stretched herself as tall as she could to put something on a top shelf. She looked back over shoulder and smiled. "Thanks," she said.

"There's fresh coffee," said Slocum. "Chuckie just brewed it up right before you drove up."

"Sounds good," she said. "I think I'll have a cup."

"Course, it ain't as good as what you make," he said, "but it ain't bad."

She laughed softly and poured a cup for herself. "Sit down at the table?" she said.

"Sure," said Slocum, and they walked into the other room and sat across from each other. Joiner came back in and took his own seat at the table. He picked up his cup and slurped from it.

"I saw Julia," Myrtle said. Joiner looked at her expectantly. "She'll be coming out."

"Did you tell her to watch out for Harman's men?" Joiner said. "Did you—"

"I told her everything," said Myrtle. "Don't worry. Us women are slicker than you men."

"Ah, now, I don't know about that," Joiner said. "I been riding around all over the place and ain't been seen yet. You got to know what you're doing to get around and keep out of sight at the same time."

"Like when you followed me to town and back?" Myrtle said.

"Like—when—"

Joiner's jaw was hanging open, and Slocum laughed.

"Chuckie," he said, "I think we better listen to the lady and believe what she says."

"Yeah," she said, and then she turned on Slocum. "And how about you?"

"I did just fine," he said. "Hell, I just went back to sleep."

"That's good," she said.

"I also had plenty of time to do some thinking," Slocum

said. He looked at Joiner. "How much ammunition do we have around here?"

"I ain't got but what's in my belt," Joiner said.

"Same here," said Slocum.

"I've got a box of shells for my Winchester," said Myrtle.

"That's good," Joiner said.

"It ain't good enough," said Slocum. "You got us set up against twenty men or more. We need to be ready for anything. Where's the nearest town to here besides Rat's Nest?"

"That'd be Flanders," Myrtle said. "It's a two-day ride over and two days back. A little longer if we have to take the wagon."

"Here's another problem," Slocum said. "I'm broke."

"I got a dollar," Joiner said.

"Well, I don't have much more than that," said Myrtle. "Not after I bought all those supplies. I've got credit at Albert's store in Rat's Nest, though. I could get whatever we need in there."

"That's no good," Slocum said. "Anyone sees you load up on ammunition in there, they'll get suspicious. We got to go to—what'd you call it?"

"Flanders?" said Joiner.

"Yeah," Slocum said. "We got to go to Flanders. Any chance of getting credit there?"

"It's too far away," Myrtle said. "I don't know anyone over there."

Slocum looked at Joiner. Joiner shrugged. "Me neither," he said.

"Well, damn it," Slocum said, "we got to do something, and right now's the time to do it, while we're waiting around for me to recuperate. And we can't go to Rat's Nest for it."

"Well," Joiner said, "what are we going to do?"

"We need ammunition," Slocum said. "We got no money to buy it. I guess we're going to have to steal it from someplace. Either that or steal some money. Any ideas?"

"I can't think of a damn thing," Joiner said. "Not without tipping our hand. And not that I could pull off by myself. If you was in shape—"

"But I ain't," Slocum said. "And when I am, we need to be ready to move."

"Wait a minute," Joiner said. "I've got an idea. There's a storage shed out on my ranch. I think that it's probably loaded with stuff. Last time I was up on the hill watching the place, I noticed quite a few cows milling around. I bet Harman will be moving them out before long. When he does, there won't be so many hands around the place. Maybe I could bust into that shed then."

Slocum thought about it for a moment. "Okay," he said. "Get back up on that hill and watch then. But be careful."

4

It was almost sundown when Joiner left to take up his watch on top of the hill. Slocum, alone again with Myrtle, sure did wish that he had his full strength back. Short of that, he longed for a good drink and a good cigar. Well, hell, he'd just have to settle for what was available. "Could we have a little coffee, Myrtle?" he asked.

"Sure," she said. "I'll get it started."

He watched her tight ass swing its way into the kitchen, and he cursed himself for having gotten shot. Another couple of days, he told himself, and I'll be all right. Then I'll do her good and proper. He heard the sound of an approaching horse just then. One horse coming at a leisurely pace. He didn't think that Joiner would be coming back so soon. He hadn't even had time to get to the top of the hill. He hurried into the bedroom for his Colt. Just as he came back out, there was a knock at the door, and Myrtle came out of the kitchen. She gave him a look, and he nodded. From where he stood, he wouldn't be seen by the visitor when she opened the door.

Myrtle moved to the door and pulled it open. Slocum could see the worried expression on her face fade, to be replaced by one of a pleasant surprise. "Julia," she said. "Come on in." Slocum lowered his Colt. Julia stepped into

31

the house, and the two women embraced. "Where's Charlie?" Julia asked.

"Gone to work," Slocum said, stepping forward. Julia gave him a surprised look.

"This is John Slocum," Myrtle said.

"Hello, John," Julia said. "Myrtle told me all about you when she came to town. I want to thank you for helping Charlie."

"Hell," Slocum said, "I ain't done nothing yet other than to just get shot."

"I'd better check the coffee," Myrtle said. "You want a cup, Julia?"

"Sure," Julia said. She turned toward Slocum as Myrtle left the room. "You said that Charlie went to work?"

"Well, yeah," Slocum said. "He went out to watch over his ranch. He thinks that Harman'll be moving some rustled beef there pretty soon, and we want to know when that happens."

"Oh," said Julia. She looked disappointed. "I came out here to see him, but I guess I'll have to wait."

"Don't blame him," Slocum said. "It was me insisted he go. I'd have done it myself, but I ain't yet quite fit. Besides, I don't know the lay of the land. We've set ourselves a big job to do, and there's just some things that can't wait."

"I understand," Julia said. "I didn't mean to sound like I was complaining."

Myrtle brought three cups of coffee out of the kitchen and put them on the table. "Come on and sit down," she said. "Both of you."

Slocum could scarcely believe that he was alone with two beautiful women, and all they were doing was sitting politely and sipping coffee. He told himself that first thing in the morning, he was going out. He would limber up his arm and shoulder, and he would saddle his horse and ride. He was tired of sitting around waiting to get better. He was going to cause it to happen. He would make himself get better.

• • •

From his station on top of the hill overlooking his lost ranch, Charlie Joiner suddenly sat up. He watched as ten cowboys saddled their horses and mounted up. He watched them ride out toward the herd on the south pasture. He knew that they were going to move the stolen cattle down into Mexico. There could be no other reason for so many cowboys to be riding out at that time of night. He watched until they were almost out of sight, and then he mounted his own horse. He turned to head back to Myrtle's house and tell Slocum what was going on, but he had a sudden change of mind. There were only two men left down at the ranch house. He sat still and studied the scene below a bit longer. One man paced the floor of the big ranch house porch. The other was out by the shed near the corral. Charlie rode easy down the hill.

At the bottom of the hill, he left his horse in some trees and moved in on the ranch on foot. Carefully working his way to the corral, he crouched against a side wall of the storage shed. Slowly he pulled out his Colt and waited. The ranch hand there paced back and forth across the front of the shed. Charlie waited until the man had come back close to the corner where he lurked. Then he sprang out and clubbed the man hard on top of the head with the butt of his Colt. The man fell like a dropped flour sack.

Not knowing how badly he had hurt the man, and not wanting to kill him while he lay there unconscious, Charlie stripped the gunbelt off the body and slung it over his own shoulder. He looked around quickly for a length of rope, found one slung over the fence, and tied the man's hands tight behind his back. Then he headed for the house. The man there had stopped pacing and was sitting in a chair, leaning back against the front wall of the house, smoking a cigarette. Charlie peeked at him from around the near corner of the house. He stepped out quickly, thumbing back the hammer of his Colt.

"Move and you're dead," he said. The man sat still.

"I ain't moving," he said.

"Stick your hands up," Joiner said. The man obeyed. "Now reach across with your left hand, real easy, and pull out that revolver and drop it." Again, the man obeyed.

Charlie walked up on the porch. About halfway to the man, he stopped, a look of surprise on his face. "Bobby?" he said.

The man turned his head to look at his captor. "Charlie," he said, and a smile spread across his face. "Charlie. By God. They said you was coming back, but I sure never thought to run into you like this. Say. You better watch out. There's a man out by the corral."

"It's all right," said Joiner. "I done met him. But what are you doing here? Are you with Harman?"

"Aw, hell, Charlie," said Bobby. "I'm working for him, all right. As a cowhand. There wasn't no other work to be had around here after you left. But if you've come to get back what's yours, you can count on me."

"I can't pay you nothing," Joiner said.

"You'll be able to later," said Bobby.

Joiner holstered his gun, and Bobby leaned over to pick up his own. He holstered it. Then he stood up and walked to meet Joiner and shake his hand. "Damn, it's good to see you," he said. "Harman's a son of a bitch. You was right about him. He's the big rustler around here. Only thing is, everyone who knows anything is either with him or afraid to say anything."

"Was there just the two of you left here tonight?" Joiner asked.

"Yeah," Bobby said. "That's all. What do you mean to do?"

"I meant to steal some ammunition and maybe some money," Joiner said, "but just now I'm getting me another idea. Where's Harman?"

"Oh, hell," Bobby said, "whenever the boys move them cattle at night, he stays in town at the Hi De Ho where everyone'll see him."

Joiner looked around. "You know," he said, "three men might could hold off twenty here at this house. What do you think?"

"Five or six would be better," Bobby said, "but, yeah, three might could. You got another man?"

"I got one," said Joiner.

"You thinking of taking it back?" Bobby asked. "Tonight?"

"Right now I've got it," said Joiner. "Ain't I?"

"You've got it," Bobby agreed.

"Only thing is," said Joiner, "I got to go back and get my man. You better come along with me in case anyone comes out here to check up on things."

"Ain't no worry about that," Bobby said. "I'll stay here and watch the place for you. If any of Harman's men should come by, I'll run them off."

Slocum heard the pounding hooves coming and went to the door with his Colt in his hand. He stepped outside and into a deep shadow to wait. The rider came in view, and he could see that it was Joiner. He lowered the Colt and stepped out. "Chuckie," he said. "What's up?"

"A change of plans, pard," Joiner said. "They moved out the herd a while ago and left only two men at the ranch. I conked one on the head and tied him up. The other one is an old friend of mine. Bobby Hale. I left him alone watching the place, but John, it's mine again. Ain't no one there but Bobby. Let's go take it over."

"Just like that?" Slocum said.

"Yeah," said Joiner. "Why not?"

"Well, hell, I don't know why not," Slocum said. "Let's do it."

They went in the house, and Joiner saw Julia right away. He called out her name and rushed over to throw his arms around her. "Julia," he said, "I been wanting to see you real bad."

"We got very little time for that," Slocum said, "if we're going to do what you said."

Julia backed off a bit and looked at Joiner in the eyes. "What?" she said. "What are you planning?"

"I got my ranch back," Joiner said. "No one's there but a friend of mine. He's watching it for me. Me and John's going down there to join him, and we'll hold it too."

"Three against twenty?" Julia said.

"Make it four," said Myrtle, going to get her rifle from the corner of the room.

"Five," Julia said. "I can shoot too."

"Well, what about your job?" Myrtle asked.

"Hell," said Julia, "it's not worth worrying about."

Joiner went back outside to saddle Slocum's horse and hitch the team to the wagon, while Slocum gathered up his few belongings and the two women packed up supplies and clothes and anything they wanted to take along with them.

"I don't have a change of clothes with me," Julia said.

"I got plenty," said Myrtle. "We're about the same size."

They loaded the wagon and tied Joiner's saddle horse on behind, and Joiner climbed up on the seat to drive. The two women joined him there. Slocum rode along beside on his big Appaloosa. It was a short ride from Myrtle's house to the big ranch house that had once belonged to Joiner. When they pulled up in front of the house, Bobby stepped out of a shadow. "Howdy," he called out. "I had to make sure it was you a-coming, Charlie."

"Good," said Joiner. "Help us unload this wagon, will you?"

"Sure," Bobby said.

"Oh, Bobby," said Joiner. "This here is John Slocum. You know the girls?"

Bobby touched the brim of his hat. "I sure do," he said. "Howdy, ladies. Pleased to meet you, Slocum." They unloaded the wagon in short order, and Bobby busied himself taking care of the horses.

"You said you hog-tied one," Slocum said.

"He's over at the corral," said Joiner.

"You ought to have killed him," Bobby said. "He's a mean one. Hell of a gunhand too."

"Okay, Boss," said Slocum, "what the hell do we do with him?"

"Well, I don't know," Joiner said. "I knocked him cold. Then I tied him up. I don't rightly know what to do with him now."

"You could kill him," said Slocum.

"When he's all helpless like that?" Joiner said.

Myrtle had stepped back out on the porch just then. She strode over to Slocum's side and pulled the revolver out of his holster. "Oh, hell," she said. "Where is he?" Joiner led her to the corral, and Slocum followed along. The man was still on the ground, still tied. He was not moving.

"Maybe you done killed him," Slocum said.

Joiner knelt beside the man and rolled him over. He leaned down close to the man's face. Then Joiner looked up. "He's alive," he said.

"Untie him," said Myrtle.

"What?"

"You heard the lady," said Slocum.

Joiner untied the wrists of the unconscious man.

"Is he right-handed or left-handed?" Myrtle asked.

"I don't know," Joiner said.

"All right then," Myrtle said. "Lay his arms out to the sides."

Joiner stretched the man's arms out straight, the palms up, and Myrtle walked over and calmly put a bullet through each palm. "Now load him on a horse and slap it on the ass," she said. "He won't do any more shooting for a long time. Maybe never." She shoved the Colt back into Slocum's holster, turned, and stalked back toward the house. Joiner stared with wide eyes at the two mangled hands.

"Get him a horse," Slocum said.

Bobby then saddled one of the ranch horses, and with the help of Joiner, loaded the still-unconscious man onto the saddle. Joiner gave the horse a slap, and it ran. "Where do you reckon he'll wind up, Charlie?" Bobby asked.

"I don't give a damn," said Joiner. "He's out of here. That's all I care about. Hey, Bobby."

"Yeah?"

"How about that Myrtle? Damn. She scares me."

"Me too," Bobby said. "I'm glad she's on our side."

"All right, boys," Slocum said, "let's get serious for a minute here. There's three of us and two women. We got to watch in all directions and be ready to get hit by twenty men."

"Eighteen," said Bobby. "Charlie knocked one out tonight."

"Charlie and Myrtle," Slocum said.

"And I was another one," Bobby added. "So there's eighteen left."

"All right," said Slocum. "Eighteen. That's still a pretty damn good crowd to have coming at you all at once. How soon do you reckon they'll be back?"

"It'll take them the best part of a week to make the trip down there, sell the cows, and then get back here," Bobby said. "It always has."

"Hey," said Joiner. "This might be the right time to hit Harman in town. Catch him short."

"How many men did you say he has in there at his saloon?" Slocum asked.

"Six or eight?" Joiner said, looking at Bobby.

"Yeah," Bobby said. " 'Bout that."

"You two going to ride in there and tackle six or eight?" Slocum said. "I ain't ready, and I don't like the odds. 'Specially on his own ground."

Joiner set a kind of a pout on his face and shoved dirt around with the toe of his boot. "I guess you're right," he said. "So what do we do then?"

"We got a week, according to Bobby here," Slocum said. "Let's hit the sack. One of us will stay awake just to be safe. We'll take turns. First daylight, we'll look around.

Check out the storehouse. Make some plans. Okay?"

"Okay," Joiner said.

"I'll take the first watch," said Slocum. "The way I've been lately, once I hit the hay, I'll be hard to get up."

"I'll head for the bunkhouse," Bobby said.

"You'll stay in the big house with the rest of us," Joiner said.

"Well, okay," said Bobby. "I'll just run over there and get my gear."

Slocum and Joiner walked together to the front porch of the big house, and Slocum set the chair in a comfortable place from which to watch. "I don't suppose there's any cigars in the house," he said.

"I'll check," Joiner said.

Slocum pulled out his Colt and reloaded the two chambers that Myrtle had emptied into the palms of the unfortunate gunnie at the corral. He reholstered it. The night was quiet and dark. He could hear crickets calling for their mates. In the distance a coyote howled and an owl hooted. The sky was clear, and the stars were bright, but the moon was only a sliver, not enough to give much light to the night sky. He heard the door open behind him, and turned to see Joiner coming back out. He had three cigars in his hand. He held them out for Slocum. Slocum looked at them and sniffed them.

"Ole Harman's got pretty good taste," he said.

Joiner handed him some matches, and he stuck all but one in his shirt pocket along with the two extra cigars. Then he reached down to strike the match on the porch floor, and he held the flame to the end of his cigar and puffed to get it going. "Ah," he said. "It's been too damn long. Thanks, pard."

Bobby came walking up with a bedroll over his shoulder. "Okay, Boss," he said to Joiner. "You going to show me where to bunk?"

"Come on," said Joiner. "John, I'll be out in two hours. That okay?"

"That's fine, Chuckie," Slocum said, and he puffed happily on his cigar.

Bobby gave Joiner a curious look. "Chuckie?" he said.

"Ah, shut up," Joiner said. "Come on in the house."

Slocum poked the cigar into his mouth and stood up. He stretched both arms out to his sides. It hurt some. He brought them back in and did it again. Then he pulled his Colt. That hurt too, and he was slow. He did it again. And again. He could see that this wasn't going to be fast or easy, but he knew that he had to get his strength and his motion back as fast as possible. He only hoped that it would be fast enough. A week, Bobby had said. They had a week to get ready for what was likely to be one hell of a fight. He stretched his arms out again. It still hurt.

5

Slocum felt a little guilty, rousing Joiner out of bed the next morning. After all, he said to himself, the poor boy hadn't seen his little Julia for something like two years. Last night had been a hell of an important night for the two of them. Still, it had to be done. According to Bobby, the cowhands would be back in about a week. There was a lot to be taken care of. Finally, everyone had crawled out of bed. Bobby was the only one who did not have to get up early. He had taken the last watch and was already up. Myrtle and Julia set about making breakfast for all of them. As soon as the coffee was ready, the men gathered around the table and sat down.

"What the hell did we have to get up so damn early for anyhow?" Joiner complained with a pout on his face. "That damn crew of old Harman's won't be back here for another week yet."

"Likely you're right about that," Slocum said. "But we want to be ready for them when they come, don't we? And what if they do show up early and surprise us? Huh? Or if the men from town decide to come out here for some reason? What about that?"

"Yeah," Joiner said. "Yeah. Hell. I guess you're right. You always are, you bastard. I just—"

"I know what you just," Slocum said. Right then Julia brought out some eggs on a platter. Slocum gave her a quick glance, enough for him to see that she sure did look good. "And I don't blame you," he added.

When they'd all finished their breakfasts, Slocum suggested that they go on outside and visit the storehouse. That was, after all, the reason Joiner had sneaked onto the ranch in the first place. It had been their first objective. They found the storehouse door padlocked, but Bobby quickly took care of that small problem. He fetched a sledgehammer from around the corner of the shed and with one mighty swing broke the lock. Then he shoved open the door, and they all went inside.

"God A'mighty," Joiner said. "Will you just look at all that shit? Man, this sure beats going to the store."

"It looks like a small arsenal," Slocum said. "That gives me an idea. Let's take all the shells into the house where they'll be handy for us. And when we've got that done, let's take some of these extra rifles and revolvers and poke their barrels out of windows—in the house, in the bunkhouse. All over the damn place."

"I get it," Bobby said. "A big bluff. Anyone comes riding up, it'll look like we got a small army here waiting for them here."

"A small arsenal for a small army," Joiner said. "Let's do it, by God. And hey, looky here." He pointed to two cases of dynamite on the floor. "That shit could come in right handy, don't you think?" he said.

"Yeah," said Slocum, slowly scratching the side of his face. "I believe it could. Take one of them into the house."

"What about the other one?" Joiner said.

"I got an idea for that too," Slocum said. "We'll use it outside."

Lugging boxes of ammunition into the house, and guns into the house and the bunkhouse, took them most of the morning, but when they were done, gun barrels protruded

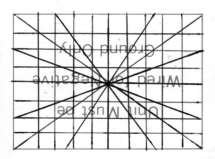

Unit Must be
Wired to Negative
Ground Only

DO NOT PUSH
TRANSMIT BUTTON
Without First Connecting
a 50 Ohm Antenna
or Dummy Load

WARNING

THIS POWER CORD IS FOR 12VOLTS DC

This transceiver is negative ground electrical systems. Simply connect the Red(fused) lead in this power cord to the positive (+) side of the 12 volt electrical system (battery pos.), and the Black lead to the negative (—) side of the electrical system (battery neg.). Refer to instruction book for complete information.

from windows on all four sides of the house, upstairs and down, and from windows on all four sides of the bunkhouse. Extra ammunition was handy in each room of the house. Slocum walked around the big house looking. Then he walked to the bunkhouse and did the same. As he came back around to the front of the bunkhouse, Joiner met him there.

"Well," Joiner said, "what do you think?"

"It might fool them," Slocum said.

"I think it looks pretty damn convincing," Joiner said.

"We'll find out," said Slocum. He looked up into the sky to see the sun almost directly overhead. "Lunchtime?" he asked.

After lunch, they went back to work. Slocum had them all busy tying the dynamite sticks from the shed into bundles of two. Then he pointed out various spots outside around the house where Bobby dug holes about six inches deep. Joiner then placed a bundle of two sticks into each hole. Finally, as Bobby put the dirt back into the holes, Joiner jabbed a short wooden stick with a strip of white cloth tied to its top into the ground to mark the spot. About halfway around, Joiner looked at Slocum.

"You sure this will work?" he said.

"If you don't trust me," Slocum said, "try one."

"Right now?" Joiner said.

"Sure," said Slocum. "Try it."

He turned and walked casually back toward the house. Joiner watched him for a moment, then looked at Bobby. Bobby shrugged. "Hand me that rifle, Bobby," Joiner said. Slocum stepped up onto the porch, then turned to watch. Joiner raised the rifle and took careful aim at the spot marked farthest to his left. Bobby looked nervous. He started toward the porch, slowly at first, then he broke into a run just as Joiner pulled the trigger. The rifle shot was followed instantly by a tremendous blast, and Joiner was bowled over backward by the force of the impact. Bobby dropped on his face just before he would have reached the porch. Myrtle and Julia came running out onto the porch.

"What was that?" Myrtle said.

"Charlie?" Julia called out.

"He's all right," Slocum said.

Bobby slowly raised his head and looked around. Then he stood up and brushed the dirt off the front of his clothes. "Goddamn," he said. "That was a hell of a blow."

Just then Julia had reached the side of the fallen Joiner. "Charlie?" she said, and Joiner sat up slowly shaking his head. Dirt fell from his head and shoulders. He had almost been buried by the huge shower of dust that had fallen on him. "Charlie," Julia said. "Are you all right?"

Back on the porch Myrtle said, "What the hell happened?"

"You're right, John," Joiner said. "Son of a bitch works fine."

Everyone got a good laugh out of that, and when they had finally quieted down again, Slocum said, "Now you need to put two more sticks back over there. That's a strategic spot."

"Come on," Julia said to Joiner. "Let's get you cleaned up."

Slocum sat in a chair near a front window smoking a cigar. Myrtle brought him a fresh cup of coffee and set it down on the table there beside the chair. "Thanks," he said.

She sat on the floor and leaned an arm on his thigh. "Where's Bobby?" she asked.

"Oh, he's out watching the road," Slocum said. "Is Chuckie boy getting his bath?"

Myrtle laughed. "Yes," she said. "There's a tub of hot water on the floor in the kitchen, and he's sitting in it. I thought I'd better get out. Julia seemed to be reaching way under the water to scrub him."

"I bet that's the best bath he's ever had," Slocum said.

Myrtle laughed again lightly. "Yeah," she said. "Maybe

it's about time I gave you a bath—another one."

"I don't remember the first one," Slocum said.

"You weren't in any shape to remember it. I remember it, though, real vividly."

"I'll bet you do."

"The tub will be available in a little while."

Slocum stretched his arm out and winced with the pain. "Not just yet," he said. "I didn't get no pile of dirt dumped all over me."

His coffee and cigar finished, Slocum went outside. He walked out to the far side of the bunkhouse. He didn't want an audience for what he was about to do. He stood loose for a moment, then pulled his Colt. It was a casual pull. He put it away and did it again. Then again. Then he braced himself, took a deep breath, and pulled fast. The Colt was only halfway up when the pain shot through his body. He grimaced with the pain and then reholstered the Colt. He pulled it easy again and again. Then fast. It still hurt, but this time he got it out and leveled it. He tried again. Okay. It wasn't as fast and easy as he'd hoped, but it was coming. He was getting it back. He kept it up for about an hour. Then he walked back to the house.

Stepping back into the main room of the big house, Slocum saw Joiner about to pour himself a glass of whiskey. The glass was on the dining table. Slocum strode quickly over, and just as Joiner poured it full, he picked it up. "Thanks," he said.

"I'll get another glass," Joiner said.

"What for?" said Slocum.

"For me," Joiner said.

"Wait till this is all over," Slocum said. "I've seen you drink. Remember?"

"Aw, hell, John," Joiner protested.

"You take a drink," Slocum said, "and I ride out of here. I mean it."

Joiner put the bottle down. "It's all right for you, though," he said.

"I'll have this one here because you already poured it," Slocum said. "That's all."

Joiner only pouted a short while. "I been thinking," he said. "Maybe one of us ought to ride in to see Sheriff Coleman. Let him know about the evidence I got on Harman."

"I been thinking about that too," Slocum said. "And I don't think so."

"Why not?" asked Joiner.

"The odds ain't good," Slocum explained. "First of all, Harman's bunch likely put you and the girls together by now. They might or might not know about me, but I ain't in any shape to be taking chances. Bobby can't go. Harman or any of his men know him, and they'd quiz him up about why he wasn't out here watching the ranch.

"Even supposing that one of us was able to get through, we ain't sure about the sheriff. You and Myrtle both said that you thought you could trust him. I didn't hear neither one of you say you was certain. That evidence of yours is too valuable to turn over to someone you ain't dead sure about.

"And let's say the sheriff is straight. Once them cowhands get back here and we run them off, I imagine that Coleman will ride out here to find out what's going on. That'll be the best way to see him. On our own ground and our own terms. You can show him what you got, but you can keep it safe in your own hands. Likely we'll find out for sure which side he's on too. Let's keep our patience and see what happens."

"John," Joiner said, "you see how come I needed you here with me so bad? You're always right. You've done kept me from doing several dumb things."

"Well, Chuckie," Slocum said, "ain't nothing happening around here just now, and you got two other men to watch out for any visitors that might show up. Seems to me it's kind of dumb of you not to be snuggling up to that little sweetie of yours."

"You're right again," Joiner said, and he left the room to find Julia. Slocum took a swig of the whiskey. It did taste good. It was just poor Joiner's dumb luck not to be able to handle a drink. He found another cigar and lit it, then with the whiskey and cigar, took up his chair by the window again. He wondered what Myrtle was doing, and he thought about going to find her, but he had already sent Joiner off to have his fun. It didn't seem like a good idea to have two of them so engaged. Just in case. Besides, he wasn't really sure that he was up to it with Myrtle yet, and he didn't want the next time to be as one-sided as the first had been.

He tried to concentrate on the problem at hand and think if there was anything they should have done that they hadn't yet taken care of, but nothing came to him. He had anticipated the return of the cowboys with a possible attack on the house, and they were ready for that. They would try to bluff the cowboys first, pointing out all the guns in the big house and the bunkhouse. They'd try to make the cowboys think they had a small army.

If the bluff didn't work, they had five guns in the house. Both women had said they could shoot. From inside the house, five ought to be able to handle twelve or so coming at them from outside. There was plenty of ammunition in the house, and it was spread around so that anyone at any window could get to plenty. There was also dynamite in the house. Sticks could be lighted and thrown if need be. And then there was the dynamite planted outside. He was pretty sure they could handle a major assault.

And then there was the business of getting the evidence to the sheriff, and Slocum was pretty sure that he had come up with the right way to deal with that issue too. He couldn't think of anything else. He finished his cigar, and the whiskey glass was empty, so he decided to go outside and find Bobby.

• • •

Upstairs in a front bedroom, Joiner was stretched out on the bed naked. Julia stood beside the bed stripping off the last of her clothes. Then she crawled up on the bed on her hands and knees and covered Joiner's body with her own. She kissed him passionately on his lips and at the same time slithered both her hands down his belly to his crotch. Her fingers crawled over his rod and his balls, and his rod sprang to sudden attention. She gripped it hard.

"Ah, there," she said. "That's what I like."

"Oh," Joiner moaned. "That's what I missed the most all this time I been gone."

"This time stay home," she said. "And watch out what you do. I thought you were blown up out there today."

"I'll be careful," he said.

"You do that," she said, and then her delicate hands guided the head of his cock in between her wet and waiting pussy lips. He moaned again out loud at the silky feeling of the walls of her cunt as she slid downward, taking his entire length up inside her. Then she leaned forward to kiss him again, and he thrust upward, driving himself as far in her as he could. She pressed down against him. He relaxed, withdrawing himself a little, then thrust upward again.

Then Julia sat up. She straightened herself, sitting down hard on Joiner's rod, her weight pressing down against his pelvis. She savored the sensation for a moment, then rocked her hips forward, then back. She rode him slowly like that for a while, then began to pick up speed. Sliding her round ass back and forth along his belly and the tops of his thighs, she rode harder and faster, until she was panting and the sweat ran down from her forehead, from her breasts, from under her arms. She was sliding on a layer of pussy juice and sweat. At last she let out a loud moan, and she shuddered all over. Then she fell forward, mashing her breasts flat against Joiner's chest.

She lay there quietly breathing deeply for a long moment. Then she kissed him again. "Oh, you're wonderful," she said.

"You're pretty damn wonderful yourself," he said, and thrust upward again and then another time.

She straightened herself up again and slid her ass forward, then back, and soon she was riding him as hard as before. This time, it didn't take half as long as it had the first, but the climax was twice as powerful. She moaned and shuddered. She twitched, and collapsed again on him.

He put his arms around her and found her to be wet all over. He kissed her neck and her cheek, and he started to thrust again. She lay still and let him for a while. Then she felt a new stir, and again she sat up, and again she rode him hard, and again she moaned and shuddered and collapsed. "God," she said, panting, "I could do this all night."

"Oh, baby," Joiner said, "I don't know if I can."

"You're doing all right," she said, and sat up and ground herself out another quick climax. Joiner could feel the juice running out of her cunt onto his flesh. He also felt the pressure building deep in his loins. He knew that it was coming, and he couldn't last much longer.

"Get yourself one more, baby," he said. She sat up and started to rock. She rode him hard again, and again she felt the wonderful shudders building up inside her, and then she felt the powerful spurt from the head of Joiner's cock, and she rocked harder and harder. She moaned and collapsed, and Joiner groaned from deep down inside himself as his cock began to soften and then then slipped out of her juicy twat.

Outside, Slocum paced under the stars. As he turned, he saw the silhouettes against the dimly lighted window of the front bedroom. He smiled. "Let him have his fun tonight," he said to himself. "We'll be deep enough into it in a few days. Won't be much time for fun then."

He thought about Myrtle and all the things he wanted to do to her, with her, and he thought about the coming fight.

He flexed his right arm. The arm still felt stiff. It would be slow healing. But the sharp pains that before had shot through his chest and side with each movement of his arm were no longer there. He moved his arm again, stretching it out to the side. He dropped it to his side and shook it, as if to shake out all the stiffness. He stood still, and he pulled out his Colt. It was a smooth pull. He dropped the revolver back into the holster, stood ready, then pulled it fast. That one was smooth too. By God, he told himself, I'm almost ready.

6

The week was up, and everyone was on alert. Slocum sat on the front porch smoking a cigar, his Winchester leaning against the wall beside him. Myrtle was in the main room of the house sitting beside a front window with a Henry rifle within her reach. Upstairs in a bedroom, Julia watched out a front window. She too had a rifle handy. Bobby was out on the road watching, and Joiner stood at a corner of the house at the far end of the porch from where Slocum sat. Everyone was tense, nervous, wondering when the cowhands would arrive, wondering how easy or how difficult it would be to drive them away.

It was early evening, but there was still some daylight left, and Bobby should be able to spot them easily and early enough to hurry back to the house and tell the others. Slocum puffed on his cigar. He was trying to figure out just how to play this hand, but he quickly decided that it would depend on how the cards were dealt. Everything would hang on how the Harman gang chose to play. There was no reason to think that they'd ride up shooting. So, if there was a chance of talking, they might be bluffed into just riding away. Of course, if it did work out that way, they'd eventually be back ready for a fight. That much was for sure.

It might be best, he thought, if they did try to take the place back. That way, Slocum and the others could pick off a few of them and lower the odds a bit before the next attack. He was pretty sure that they could drive them off this first time without much problem. The cowboys would be surprised. They were not expecting any trouble, especially not here at what they thought was their headquarters.

"Hey," Joiner called out from the corner of the house.

"I hear it," Slocum said. "It'll be Bobby."

"Then the cowhands ain't far behind," Joiner said.

"That's right," Slocum said. He puffed some more on his cigar, savoring the flavor. Bobby rode into sight. He pulled up just in front of the porch.

"They're a-coming," he said. "Ten of them, riding real casual."

"That's only two each," Slocum said. "That ain't too bad."

"Yeah," Bobby agreed, "but them ten is professional gunfighters. Mean as hell."

"Put your horse in the corral, Bobby," Slocum said, "and get back over here on the porch."

Bobby did that, and was back in a flash. Slocum stood up and moved his chair to the center of the porch, just in front of the door into the house. He brought along the Winchester, and this time, when he sat back down, he laid the rifle across his lap. "Chuckie," he said, "go back to your corner." Joiner walked back to the end of the porch to Slocum's right. "Bobby," Slocum said, "why don't you take the other end?" Bobby walked to the end of the porch to Slocum's left. Both men stepped off the porch and around the corner of the house to lean against the side wall. Soon the ten riders came.

When they had reached the line where the flagged sticks poked out of the ground, Slocum called out to them. "That's far enough," he said. The rider in the middle and a little out front of the others held up a hand, and he and the others stopped riding. He squinted at Slocum. "Who the hell are you?" he said.

"Name's Slocum. John Slocum, but that ain't what's important," Slocum said. "What's important is that this ranch is back in the hands of Charlie Joiner and his crew. You might say I'm Charlie's foreman." He stood up, rifle ready, and stepped to the front edge of the porch. "Now I'm suggesting that you fellows turn around and ride out of here if you want to avoid a bloodbath," he said. "Boss?"

Joiner stepped out from around the corner of the house and leveled his rifle at the leader. "Right here," he said.

"Bobby," said Slocum.

Bobby stepped out and aimed his rifle. "Ready," he said.

"Bobby?" said the talking cowboy. "That you?"

"It's me, all right," Bobby said.

"You with these others?"

"Sure looks that way, Herd," Bobby said.

"You're a double-crossing little shit, Bobby," said Herd, "and you're going to be real sorry when I get my hands on you."

"Call it any way you like, Herd," Bobby said. "My first boss on the ranch here was Charlie. I stayed on when you all ran him off, but now he's back. That's all."

"That's enough talking," Joiner shouted. "Now you can turn around and ride out of here or start shooting."

"Who's that?" Herd asked.

"Charlie Joiner," said Joiner. "Make your move."

Herd laughed. "Hell," he said, "there's ten of us here and three of you. How long you think a fight would last?"

"You'll be the first to fall," Slocum said, sighting in on him with his Winchester. "And before you make up your mind, look around. Look at the windows."

Herd saw the rifles then, one protruding from each window. "Turn around, boys," he said. "We'll see what Mr. Harman says about this." The other riders turned their horses, and just before turning his own, Herd shouted back at the defenders of the house, "We'll be back. You can count on that."

●   ●   ●

They kept a watch up for the rest of the evening and all through the night, but it was midmorning of the next day before anyone came back to the ranch. Slocum was in the house, when Myrtle, who had been out on the porch, stepped into the main room. "Sheriff's coming," she said.

"Alone?" Slocum asked.

"He's alone," Myrtle said. In a minute, Slocum, Joiner, Bobby, and the two women were all out on the porch. Sheriff Coleman rode up easy and stopped his mount at the hitching rail there. He looked up at the crowd waiting there to meet him.

"Mind if I get down?" he asked.

"Climb down," Joiner said.

Coleman swung out of the saddle, lapped the reins of his horse around the rail, and stepped up onto the porch. "Have a chair, Sheriff," said Joiner. Coleman sat, and so did the others, all except Myrtle.

"Coffee, Sheriff?" she asked.

"I don't mind," Coleman said.

Myrtle went into the house, and Julia got up to follow her. "I'll give you a hand," she said.

"It's been a long time, Charlie," Coleman said.

"Two years," said Joiner.

"I heard rumors that you was coming back."

"And here I am," said Joiner. "I got my ranch back too."

"Well," Coleman said, "you're in possession right now. There's no arguing with that."

"And possession's nine-tenths of the law," said Joiner. "Or something like that. Ain't it?"

"If that's so," Coleman said, "then the other tenth is papers, and it's a powerful tenth. Harman's got the papers on this place. I came out here to ask you to give it up, Charlie. I don't want no trouble with you."

"I got my ranch back," Joiner said, "and I ain't giving it up again."

Just then, Myrtle and Julia came back out and distributed

cups of coffee all around. Coleman took a tentative sip. "That's real good, ladies," he said. "Thank you."

"Bud," said Joiner, "you know that Harman stole this place from me. Now, I ain't accusing you of nothing, but why the hell would you want to help him keep it?"

"Be careful what you say, Charlie," Coleman said. "I don't know nothing of the kind. All I know is that you ran off a couple of years ago. Whenever your tax bill come up delinquent, Harman paid it. He got the ranch legal. Now you've come back and took it by force, and Harman's made a complaint. That's all I know."

"You know why I left?" Joiner said.

"I heard rumors," Coleman said. "A bunch of the ranchers got together and accused you of rustling. They was going to string you up, but you got away from them."

"That's right," said Joiner, "but I never rustled no cattle. It was Harman. He had his boys put them cows on my place, and it was him accused me, and it was his boys that got the lynch mob up. It was all part of his scheme to get my ranch away from me."

"That may be," said Coleman, "and I've had my suspicions. But there ain't no proof of any of it. The facts are just the way I laid them out for you. I'm sorry, Charlie, but you're going to have to give it up."

"Chuckie boy," said Slocum, "show the man the papers you got."

Coleman shot a glance at Slocum. "What papers?" he said. Slocum didn't answer, and Coleman looked back at Joiner. "What papers?" he said. "What's he talking about?"

Joiner reached inside his shirt and drew out a folded oilcloth. He laid it on his thigh and unwrapped it to reveal a stack of papers. Then he handed the papers to Coleman. Coleman read the top paper, then went hurriedly through the stack. He looked up at Joiner. "Harman's our rustler, all right," he said. "How'd you get all this?"

"I ain't just been idling down there south of the border," Joiner said. "Well?"

"Well, I can arrest Harman on this evidence," said Coleman, "but that won't give you back your ranch. It'll just put him in jail."

"That'd be a good start," Slocum said. "Why don't you just set aside the problem of possession of this ranch till you get Harman in jail? Then Chuckie can get it back the same way Harman got it away from him in the first place."

Coleman stroked his chin contemplatively. "We might work it like that," he said. He finished his coffee and put the cup down on the porch. "You'll be hearing from me," he said, standing up. He started toward the porch steps, but Slocum stopped him.

"Sheriff," he said, "I think that you ought to leave those papers here with us—for now."

Coleman looked at the papers in his hand, then looked from Slocum to Joiner and the others there on the porch. He was outnumbered, and clearly they were determined. "Well," he said, "I guess we won't really need them till the trial." He handed the bundle back to Joiner, then moved on to his horse. Loosening the reins, he mounted up. He looked back at the five on the porch, touched the brim of his hat, and said, "Be seeing you."

"Sheriff," Slocum said. "Be careful. From what I hear, this Harman ain't no respecter of the law."

"Don't worry about me," Coleman said. He turned his horse and rode away.

Harman sat behind the big desk in the office inside the Hi De Ho Saloon. He was a tall man, rangy and tough-looking. His hard face had a black mustache that matched the heavy brows over his eyes. His black coat and hat hung on a tree just inside the office door. He was wearing the trousers and vest that went with the coat, and he had on a white shirt with lace collar and cuffs, and a black string tie. He looked up from his work when he heard a knock on his door.

"Come in," he called out.

The door opened and Sheriff Bud Coleman stepped in.

"Well?" said Harman. "You bring them in?"

"They wouldn't listen to reason, Harman," Coleman said. "And I was outnumbered. Five of them met me on the porch, and there were rifles poking out every window of the house. The bunkhouse too. Charlie Joiner's got a small army out there."

"Then we've got to get together a bigger one," said Harman, "and drive them out of there or kill them."

"Wait a minute," said Coleman. "There'll be time enough for that later. Just now, I'd like for you to come along with me."

"Come along where, Bud?" Harman said.

"Over to the jailhouse," said Coleman. "I got to put you under arrest."

Harman leaned back in his chair and looked at the sheriff in disbelief. "There's a known rustler in possession of my ranch illegally," he said, "and you want to put me under arrest? Just what the hell for?"

"Suspicion of cattle rustling," Coleman said.

"Well, now," Harman said, taking a cigar out of a box on his desk and sticking it in his mouth. "Just what is it makes you suspicion me?" He picked up a match and struck it on the side of the desk, then stuck the flame to the end of the cigar.

"I got a look at some bills of sale from south of the border," Coleman said. "They show that you've been selling the cattle that's been rustled from around here."

"Let me see the papers," Harman said.

"I ain't got them on me," Coleman said. "I ain't that stupid. You'll get to see them soon enough. You or your lawyer."

"Wait a minute," said Harman. "Let me work this out here. I sent you out to the ranch to get Charlie Joiner out of there, and you come back with a story about some papers that prove me a rustler. Is that right? To the best of my knowledge, Joiner's been down in Mexico for the last couple of years. That all adds up to one thing. Joiner showed you them papers. Am I right?"

"That'll be answered at your trial," the sheriff said. "Come on, Harman. Don't give me any shit."

"Them papers is fake," Harman said. "Bring them in here and let's have them examined."

"They'll be examined by the judge," Coleman said. "Come on now. Let's go."

Harman spread his arms to his sides in a gesture of submission. "All right," he said. He stood up and walked around his desk to the hat tree, then took his coat and started to put it on. "I'll go. I'm a law-abiding citizen. We'll get this all straightened out, and come next election, if you last that long, you'll be voted out of office."

"We'll see," said Coleman, taking the black hat off the tree and setting it on Harman's head. "Let's go."

As they walked through the big main room of the Hi De Ho Saloon, the man called Herd turned away from the bar and straightened up. As the sheriff and Harman walked past him, Harman said, "Keep an eye on things, Herd. The sheriff's putting me in jail." Then Harman walked on out the front door along with Coleman. Herd stared after them for a moment, then gestured toward two cowboys sitting at a table close by. They stood up and walked over to the bar to join him.

"Kurt," Herd said, "you and Jelly come along with me."

Herd led the two other men out of the saloon and down the street to the sheriff's office and jail. They stepped inside just as Coleman was about to shut a cell door on Harman. Herd pulled a revolver, and the other two men did the same. "Hold it, Sheriff," Herd said. Coleman stopped still.

"Harman," the sheriff said, "is this the way you want it?"

"It's the only way," Harman said. "You don't really think I'd sit in your damned jail waiting for a trial, do you?"

Just then Deputy Joe Short stepped in the door behind Herd and the other two. Taking in the situation quickly, he pulled out his revolver.

"Well, what now, boys?" said Coleman. Short edged his way between Kurt and Jelly to stand beside Herd. "Joe, you damn fool," said Coleman, "you left two men at your back."

"Way I see it, Mr. Harman," Short said, "there's only one thing to do now."

"Do it then," Harman said.

Coleman's eyes opened wide with the sudden realization, too late, of where his deputy's loyalties lay. "Joe?" he said. "Joe, you no-good son of a bitch."

Joe Short's revolver barked and jumped in his hand, and a bullet tore into the chest of Sheriff Bud Coleman. Coleman's right hand had just touched the handle of his own revolver. He never had a chance to grip it. He groaned angrily and looked down at the fresh hole in his chest. Blood ran freely down onto the belly of his shirt. "No good—" His voice faded, and his knees buckled, and Coleman crumpled to the floor.

"Well, Joe," Harman said, "I guess that makes you the law around here."

"What about Eddie?" Short asked.

"If Eddie Cobb is willing to string along with us," said Harman, "then I reckon he can keep his job as deputy— your deputy. Take these two along with you. Find him and feel him out. Then look me up over at the Hi De Ho. We got things to do."

"All right, Mr. Harman," Short said.

Back at the ranch, Slocum walked the row of buried dynamite sticks. The gang of cowhands had trampled some of the flag sticks, and he wanted to straighten them up, make sure the targets were all clear and plain. He figured they might be needing them before much longer. With the power that Harman had behind him, Slocum couldn't imagine that the man would just calmly walk into a jail cell and let himself be locked up to wait for a trial on a cattle-rustling charge. Harman had wanted what he considered his ranch back before. Now he was going to want it that much harder and faster.

Ten men, Slocum thought. And what had they said about the ones in town? Six more, was it? That would be sixteen all told. Sixteen coming at them. They had to be ready.

Joe Short led Jelly and Kurt across the street to the Long Shank Hotel, where Eddie Cobb had a room. He figured Eddie might be in there. They were approaching the front door when Cobb came hurrying out. "Hey, Eddie," Short said. "We was just coming to see you."

"I heard a shot," Cobb said.

"It's all right," said Short. "I took care of it. We got to talk, Eddie. Come on over to the Hi De Ho and let's talk over a glass of whiskey."

"Well, okay," Cobb said.

They walked to the Hi De Ho, and got themselves a table in a far corner away from other customers. Kurt got them a bottle and four glasses, and Short poured drinks all around. "What's this all about?" Cobb asked.

"Eddie," Short said, "Bud went and got himself killed."

"What? That shot I heard—"

"That was it," Short said. "Sit still and listen to me. You know, Charlie Joiner and his gang have took over Mr. Harman's ranch out there."

"Yeah," Cobb said. "I heard about that."

"Mr. Harman asked Bud to run them off or arrest them, but Bud come back in town and said he was fixing to arrest Mr. Harman for rustling," Short said. He turned down his drink and poured himself another. "On Joiner's word," he added.

Eddie Cobb looked at Short's cold face, and he looked at the two Harman men who were siding Short.

"That's slim," he said.

"Yeah," said Short. "So Mr. Harman said he figures that I'm the sheriff now. What he actually said was that I'm the only law. I said what about Eddie, and he said if Eddie strings along with us, he can keep his job—as deputy. So what I'm asking you, Eddie, is where do you stand?"

"You mean—whose side am I on?" Cobb asked.

"That's what I mean to know," said Short.

Cobb sipped some whiskey and thought carefully about the words he would use. "Well," he said, "it was Bud who hired me. Now you're sheriff, I'd say it was up to you whether you want me or not. I mean, Bud got to choose his own deputies. You ought to have the same right. If you don't want me, I'll move on. No hard feelings."

"It ain't that," Short said. "I'm asking you, if I keep you on, will you stick by me?"

"Does that mean sticking by Mr. Harman?" Cobb asked.

"The way I see it," said Short, "the law's on Mr. Harman's side."

Cobb lifted his glass for another sip. "Well," he said, "I don't know nothing about the law. All I know is—if I work for a man, I do what he tells me to do. So if you're the new sheriff, I got no quarrel with that. It ain't my place to decide whose side the law's on. Just do what I'm told. That's all."

"You just keep thinking like that, Eddie," Short said, "and we'll all get along just fine. Now, uh, why don't you get on over to the office and clean things up there. I'll see you later."

Short, followed by Kurt and Jelly, headed toward Harman's office, and Eddie Cobb walked out the front door. He walked over to the sheriffs office and found the body of Bud Coleman lying there on the floor. He looked out the front door and didn't see any of Harman's men watching, but he didn't want to take any chances. He headed for the back door, but paused as he came to the sheriff's body. He took off his hat and looked down.

"Sorry to run out on you like this, Bud," he said, "but I'll be back. I promise you that."

He put his hat back on his head and hurried to the rear door. He went out and walked down the back alley until he came to the livery. He entered the livery from its back door, got his horse and saddled it up, and rode out the back way. He was headed for the ranch and the so-called Joiner gang.

7

The sun was just going down, and Slocum was standing his watch out on the front porch of the big ranch house when he saw the lone rider coming down the lane. He jacked a shell into the chamber of the Winchester just in case and waited until the man was well within shouting range. "Hold up there," he called out. "Who are you and what do you want here?" The rider stopped his horse.

"The name's Eddie Cobb," the rider shouted. "Sheriff's deputy. I want to talk to Charlie Joiner. That's all. Just talk."

"Hold your hands away from your sides and ride on in— slow and easy," Slocum said.

Cobb urged his horse forward and rode with his hands up and out to his sides to make it clear that he was not a threat. He was getting closer to the porch when Joiner and Bobby came out the door, having heard the shouts. A minute later the two women came out to join them. Cobb rode up close to the porch and stopped his horse. "Eddie," said Joiner. "What are you doing here?"

"They killed Bud," said Cobb. "Can I step down?"

"Oh, God," said Julia. "I was afraid of that."

"Come on down," Slocum said, lowering his Winchester. "Come and sit with us."

"Goddamn," said Joiner. "I should have known. I should—"

"Never mind all that," Slocum said. "Coleman was a hardheaded lawman. None of us could have stopped him from trying it his way."

Cobb stepped up on the porch and took the chair that Myrtle offered him. The others gathered chairs from various places on the porch and pulled them all together in a circle.

"Tell us what happened," Slocum said.

"I don't know exactly," said Cobb. "I knew that Bud had come out here, and I knew why. Later, I was up in my room at the hotel, and I heard a shot. I was coming out the front door of the hotel to investigate when Joe Short met me. He had two of Harman's men with him, and he said that Bud was dead and he was sheriff. He wanted to talk. I went on over to the Hi De Ho with them and, well, I can't recall just exactly what he said, but what it amounted to was that if I would go along with them, I could stay on as deputy.

"I figured that I'd better play along with them right then if I wanted to stay alive, so I allowed as how I wouldn't be bothered by nothing long as I had my job. Joe told me to go take care of things in the office. I went over there and found Bud. I reckon that's what Joe meant. He meant for me to take care of the body. Well, poor old Bud had been shot once through the chest. His gun wasn't even out of the holster. I couldn't think what to do except come on out here. I sure won't have no truck with Harman and that bunch. If you all don't want me, I guess I'll just have to get out of the country. I can't stay in Rat's Nest."

"Did Short say anything else?" Slocum asked.

"No, I don't think so," said Cobb. "Wait a minute. Yeah. He said that Harman had complained that you all was out here illegal, so Bud had come out to take care of things, but then he had come back to town and made out to arrest Harman instead. That's what he said."

"Well," Julia said, "I guess we know now where Joe Short stands."

"You all want me here?" Cobb asked. "If it comes to a showdown, I can handle a gun all right."

Slocum glanced at Joiner. "You're the boss here, Chuckie boy," he said. "Answer the man."

"Huh? Oh, yeah," Joiner said. "Well, sure. Glad to have you, Eddie. Hell, we need all the help we can get."

"That's for sure," Slocum said, "I expect we'll get an all-out attack just any time now. Especially when they discover that Eddie here has slipped out on them."

"Will they attack at night?" Julia asked.

"No telling what they'll do," Slocum said. "If I was to have to guess, I'd say in the morning, but we better watch through the night to be safe. Chuckie boy, you'd better tell ole Eddie here about the stakes out there in the yard. I'm going to turn in and get some sleep. Big times coming."

It was ten o'clock the next morning when Bobby, watching from the porch, sounded the alarm and ran back into the house to take up a post at a front window. Slocum was at the other window of the main room in another instant. Joiner headed for the stairs. "Come with me, Eddie," he said, and the two of them ran up to the second floor.

Slocum watched through the window as the large force of gunmen rode into the yard. Coming out of the narrow lane, they spread themselves out there in front of the house. Herd was in the lead, in the center, as the rest moved to the sides. The man to his immediate right wore a badge on his vest. Slocum figured that one to be Joe Short. Herd raised a rifle and aimed at one of the lower windows. Slocum made a quick count. Fifteen men.

"This is the only chance you'll get," Herd shouted. "Come out with your hands up, and you won't get hurt. Resist and we'll blast you all to pieces."

"You go to Hell, you pig-shit son of a bitch," Joiner yelled, and he squeezed off a round that tore a chunk out of Herd's left ear. Blood flew out from the wound as Herd yelped in surprise and pain and fired a wild shot that thudded harmlessly into the front wall of the house. Slocum took careful aim and knocked Herd backwards out of his saddle. All of a sudden everyone on both sides was shooting. The glass in all the front windows was shattered. Lamps and vases were blasted, and the walls in the rooms were pockmarked.

As Joe Short was raising his rifle to take aim, a bullet smacked into his forehead, knocking his head back. He rocked in his saddle for a moment before toppling off to one side. One bold rider decided to make a desperate charge for the house. Kicking his mount viciously and riding hard, he raised a six-gun and headed straight for the center of the porch as if he would ride right up on it and in through the front door. From his window post, Bobby shot the man through the face, and the horse, suddenly riderless, raced around in confused circles.

Then Slocum noticed that four riders were huddled close together to his far right. Near them a flagged stick poked up out of the ground. He took careful aim and fired, and the earth was rocked by the tremendous explosion that followed. One horse and rider flew up into the air. Another horse was knocked off its feet, pinning its rider's leg under its body. The other two riders were thrown and their frightened horses ran loose. Through the dust and debris and smoke, Slocum could see the remaining members of the Harman gang racing toward cover back at the end of the lane, some on foot, some still mounted and riding hard.

Eddie Cobb, from an upstairs window, took aim at the laggard of the bunch, who was running on foot as fast as he could. Cobb squeezed his trigger, and he could see his shot tear into the man's ass. The man fell forward and squirmed helplessly there on the ground. Then he started screaming in pain and fright. "Don't leave me here!" he shouted. "Help me. Someone come back and help me. You bastards.

I'm shot. Don't leave me here, you chickenshits. I'm shot in the ass."

Suddenly everything was still and quiet. Slocum watched. Myrtle came up behind him. "Are they gone?" she asked.

"I think so," he said. "I ain't sure. Fetch Bobby for me."

Myrtle went for Bobby, and soon the two of them were there with Slocum. Slocum stood up. "Bobby," he said, "let's me and you go out there and see what's what."

"I'm game," said Bobby.

Slocum led the way to the front door. He stood to one side, turned the knob, and shoved the door wide open. No shots were fired. "Come on," he said. He went out the door and stepped quickly to his left. Bobby came out behind him and stepped to the right. Still no shots were fired. They walked on down into the yard, where the air was filled with smoke and the smell of burned black powder, and made their way first to the man pinned under his horse. He saw them coming and raised his hands. "Don't shoot," he said. "I'm helpless here. I can't get up, and I think my leg's broke."

Slocum said, "Get his guns, Bobby." Bobby took the man's guns and tossed them aside. Then he and Slocum started making their way slowly across to the other side of the yard, where the lane came in.

"Hey," said the man with the broken leg, "what about me?" The butt-shot man was still writhing, once again whining and begging for help. Bobby kicked the man's guns out of his reach and walked on by.

They found no men in the scraggly woods along the sides of the lane. All the other survivors had fled. Slocum and Bobby walked back into the yard, and Slocum made his way over to the butt-shot man. He toed him over onto his back, and the man screamed with pain at the movement. Slocum looked down to see where the bullet had come out. The man's crotch was blood-soaked. Slocum pulled his Colt and put a bullet in the man's chest. Bobby looked at him in clear astonishment. "Hell," said Slocum, "he wouldn't never have been good for nothing again, shot where he was. Let's gather up the loose horses and pick up all the guns."

By this time the others had come out of the house to look around. Joiner ran quickly over to Slocum's side. "We whipped them, John," he said. "We did it. Goddammit, we whipped their ass."

"This time," said Slocum. "It ain't over."

While Slocum, Joiner, Bobby, and Cobb caught the stray horses, put them in the corral, and unsaddled them, Myrtle and Julia picked up rifles and six-guns and carried them into the house. That done, Slocum took a cigar out of his pocket and lit it. Joiner stepped over by his side. Looking around at the bodies strewn about the yard, he said, "What're we going to do with these?"

"Count them," Slocum said. "Then load them up in the wagon. We'll send them back where they come from."

Joiner grinned. "Yeah," he said. "That's a good idea. Send them home to Harman and let him worry about burying them."

They found seven bodies and loaded them up. Then Slocum said, "Drag that son of a bitch over there out from under his horse."

They did, the man screaming in pain the whole time. "You're tearing my leg off," he cried. Then they tied the dead horse to the back of the wagon, and they heaved the man with the broken leg up onto the wagon seat. "Ah," he cried out. "You're killing me."

"Shut up," said Slocum. "We could, but we ain't. Take this wagon into Rat's Nest and tell your boss that we're still here. If you're lucky, maybe he'll get someone to set your broke leg for you. Maybe you'll walk again."

"I can't drive like this," the man said. "I'm in terrible pain."

"If you can't drive," Slocum said, "then we'll kill you. We got no other reason to let you live."

Wincing in pain, the man flicked the reins, and the wagon lurched forward. With the extra drag on the rear, the team pulled slowly, but the wagon rolled, and finally it was out of sight down the road toward Rat's Nest. Slocum took a puff on his cigar. "Let's all sit down and talk this over now," he said.

They sat in the chairs on the porch, and Myrtle and Julia served coffee all around. Slocum puffed on his cigar, savoring the fine flavor. "Well, we killed seven," he said, "and we put one more out of commission. How many has Harman got left?"

"There was twenty to start with," Myrtle said. "Subtract two right from the first. Bobby here and the one whose hands I shot."

"Eighteen," said Bobby. "We killed seven here this morning. And Bobo, him with the broke leg, he ain't no good. That's eight. So there's only ten left."

"One of them seven was Joe Short," said Eddie Cobb. "There's still eleven. Eleven and Harman himself."

"So it's us against twelve," Slocum said.

"Hell," said Joiner. "There's six of us here. That's only two apiece. That ain't bad."

"We were lucky here today," Slocum said. "As many bullets as flew through the windows a while ago, it's a wonder none of us was hit. We might could hold them off again like that, if we have to, but I'd sure like to come up with something else. I'd sure like to have a better plan."

Harman was sitting at a table in the Hi De Ho Saloon when the four battered riders pounded up out in the street. He waited there until the men came staggering into the saloon, and when he saw that there was only four of them, and those looking like whipped dogs, a worried look crossed his weathered face. "Where the hell's the rest of the boys?" he said. "Damn it. Where's Herd?"

"Herd's killed," said Jelly, one of the lucky survivors. "Deader'n hell. Joe Short too. Hell, Boss, they got a army out there, and some kind of explosives. It was like war. A goddamn war. I ain't kidding you. We're lucky to have got away alive with our skins on us."

"Are you four the only ones left?" Harman said.

"I think there's some more," Jelly said. "I don't know how many, but they're on foot. They'll be coming along."

"Goddammit," Harman said. He turned to the man sitting to his right. "When the rest get in here, come and tell me," he said. "I'll be in my office."

As Harman stomped across the room and on into his office and slammed the door, Jelly sat down at the table in the seat Harman had just vacated. "Well, I don't know about the rest of you boys," he said, "but I sure need myself a drink. I ain't never been through the like of that before. Never."

The other three sat down and soon whiskey was poured all around. They'd had a couple of rounds each when the wagon pulled up outside. Jelly jumped up and ran to the door. "Goddamn, would you look at this?" he said. The others soon crowded around him, then shoved their way through the door to gather around the wagon there in the street. The wagon was hauling three healthy men, one hurt man, and seven bodies. It was also dragging a dead horse. Jelly turned to the man, who had been sitting beside Harman earlier in the saloon. "You better go get the boss," he said. "He'll need to see this, his own self, in person. Ain't no way for any of us to go describe it to him. Just no way."

The broken-legged man then yelled from the back of the wagon. "Somebody get me out of here," he said. "Get me to a doc. Get me off these damn dead men."

In another moment, the broken-legged man was dragged screaming off the pile of bodies and helped away somewhere, presumably to a doctor's office. Then the messenger came back out of the saloon with Harman. Harman looked at the bodies in the bed of the wagon. He looked at the dead horse. "Holy shit," he said. "How many men they got out there anyhow?"

"I don't know," said Jelly, "but they was shooting out of every damn window in that big house. You know, your house."

Kurt was just climbing down off the wagon bench. "They was shooting a fucking cannon at us too." he said, "Or something. Blowed over four horses. Blowed one horse right up into the air. Horse and rider. I seen it. Well, we took off. Some of us on foot, some still on horseback. The bastards on horse just run off and left us. We was walking along the road, dragging ass, when Bobo come along driving this stink wagon. His leg was all busted up. His horse had fell on him, he said, and they had just went and drug him out from under it and then made him drive this nasty load to town. Well, we put him in the back and clumb on up, and here we are."

"All right," Harman said. "All right. You men go on inside and get yourselves a drink, a bath, whatever you need. Jelly, you and Kurt come along with me. We got some figuring to do."

Slocum struggled with his thoughts. He was trying to decide on the best move to make next. If their calculations were right, they had reduced the size of the enemy force almost in half. That much was good. There was really no way of knowing, though, if Harman had the means of raising more gunfighters. Even if he did, it would take some time. So if they could act fast enough, they'd have the dozen men to deal with, no more. On the Joiner side, they had four men and two women. The women were both good shots, but Slocum didn't like the idea of using them any more than he had to, and certainly not for any kind of a face-to-face showdown.

He was trying to decide which of three or four approaches to the problem would be best. Should they just stay put and wait for the next assault by Harman's men? They had done well enough against the first attack, but a second one would be different. Harman's bunch now knew what was waiting for them at the ranch house. When they came back, they would likely sneak in, maybe come at the house from all sides, try to get up to and even into the house before anyone was able to detect their presence. It wouldn't be easy to watch all possible approaches to the house. It would be a very different kind of a fight.

A second possibility that occurred to Slocum was the laying of an ambush somewhere between the ranch and the town of Rat's Nest. If they could set up a sentry somewhere along the way who would spot any approach of Harman's bunch, then, when he brought the word that they were on the way, Slocum, and his friends could plant themselves along the road and blast the bastards from ambush. If they were to try that, though, Slocum would insist that the women be left out of the fight. There would then be only four guns against the Harman gang, however many Harman should choose to send out, up to twelve. And if anything should go wrong, if the Harman gang should prevail, the two women would be left alone back at the ranch house. He didn't like that thought.

He had one other thought, and he called the rest of the party together out on the porch to discuss it. First he explained to them the problems of the first two possibilities as he saw them, and everyone seemed to agree with him on their drawbacks, except for the two women, who disagreed when Slocum talked about being protective of them. "We can handle ourselves," Myrtle said. Slocum let that slide and went on.

"So here's the other way we can go," he said. "But we need to start right now. We need to hit them while they're licking their wounds. I don't think we ought to ride like an army into town and attack the saloon. That'd be the quickest way to get the rest of the town on Harman's side. We'd look like an outlaw gang riding in on a raid or something. I don't think we should do that.

"But here's what we could do. We could go in, just one or two of us at a time, and take out one or two of them wherever we could find them. We'd have to figure out where to find them when they ain't all together. Take out one or two here, another one there, until we get them whittled down to size. Now, you all know the lay of the land. I don't. And some of you ought to know something about their habits. So what do you say?"

"I think we could get to them easy enough right now," Joiner said. "Like you said, they're licking their wounds. Ain't likely to be anyone watching the trails for us either."

"Harman has a room upstairs in the Hi De Ho," said Eddie Cobb. "For nights when he didn't want to ride back out here. He'd be either in that room, or downstairs in the saloon, or in his office. Any way you look at it, he's in that building somewhere. And he'll keep at least two gunhands there with him all the time. Kurt and Jelly each have rooms in the hotel. It's across the street and down to the south from the saloon. Course, the cowhands had all been staying out here. I don't know where they'll be put up."

"Has the Hi De Ho got extra rooms upstairs?" Slocum asked.

"Well, yeah," said Cobb. "I guess you could call them that. They've got whores in them."

"Well, then," Slocum said, "we'd most likely find most of the gang in the same building, unless they'd gone out somewhere to eat or were on their way out here."

"Most likely," Cobb said. "Course, there ain't no guarantee."

"There never is," said Slocum. He stuck a cigar in his mouth and rolled it around. "We don't want to leave this place unguarded," he said. "We don't think they'll be coming out here right away, but we can't be sure of that either. What do you all say to this notion? Let me and Eddie here slip into town and see just how much damage we can do real quiet-like. That way the rest of you will be here guarding the house, and if anything happens to us in town, you'll still have possession here."

"I don't like it," Myrtle said. "Just the two of you in town alone? It's too dangerous."

"The only thing that ain't dangerous," Slocum said, "would be if we was all to pack up and run for it right now. Short of that, we got to do something, and anything we do will have its risks. But I ain't trying to ramrod things here. I'll listen to any ideas anybody else has."

They sat quietly. Finally Eddie Cobb said, "Slocum, let's me and you go to town."

8

Slocum and Cobb tied their horses in a clump of trees just outside Rat's Nest. The sun had just gone down, and the small grove was in heavy shadow. They were behind a small frame house, and from inside the house, light showed through one window. "Harvey Beard lives in there," Cobb said in a low voice. "Likely he's alone. He's there, or else there wouldn't be no light."

"How come you're so sure he's alone?" Slocum asked.

"I know his habits," said Cobb. "He plays around in the Hi De Ho, but when he goes home, he goes alone. Always has."

"Okay," Slocum said. "Let's go get him."

They made their way quietly and cautiously to the front door of the house. Slocum pressed himself against the wall to the side of the door, took out his Colt, and nodded. Cobb knocked on the door. "Who's there?" called Beard's voice from in the house.

"Harvey," said Cobb, "open up."

"Who is it?" Beard demanded.

"It's Eddie. Eddie Cobb. Open up."

The door was jerked open, and Harvey Beard stood there with a gun in his hand. He glared at Cobb. "Where the fuck have you been?" he asked.

Looking at the gun, Cobb backed away a few steps. "Hiding out," he said. "Harvey, you don't need that gun. I just want to talk to you. That's all. Hey, I didn't come after you with my gun out, did I?"

"I ain't got nothing to talk to you about, but I damn sure bet Mr. Harman would like to have a talk with you," Beard said, and he stepped out the door moving toward Cobb. Slocum swung his arm fast and hard, bringing his heavy Colt down on Beard's right wrist. They could all hear the sound of a bone snapping. Beard felt it, and he yowled in pain and fright. His gun fell to the ground. Cobb reached down to pick it up as Slocum grabbed Beard's shirtfront with his left hand and slammed him against the wall. He poked the barrel of his Colt against Beard's nose.

"Ow," said Beard. "Oh. Goddammit. You broke my goddamn arm. Ow. Shit. What'd you do that for?"

"To save your worthless life, you dumb shit," Slocum said. "This way you won't be no good for Harman. And there's a big fight coming. For your own good, I suggest you pack up and get out of the country."

"How can I pack with this arm broke?" Beard said.

"That's your problem," said Slocum. "Would you rather get killed? We can sure enough oblige you if that's what you want."

"No," said Beard. "No. Hell. I'll get out. Ain't nothing here that I need anyhow. I don't need to pack nothing. I just wish I could see a doctor first, but that's all right. I'll go. I'll go. Shit. You broke me up real good, you don't need to be killing me."

"I'll saddle his horse," said Cobb.

"You mean I got to ride out right now?" Beard whined, wincing with pain. "With this arm the way it is?"

Cobb went to get the horse ready, and Slocum shoved Beard harder against the wall. "No," Slocum said. "You don't have to go. But if you stay, I'll kill you. How many times do I have to explain things to you?"

"All right, all right," Beard said. "I'll go. I'll go right

now, but you've probably ruined me for life. I hope you know that."

"Likely so," Slocum said. "At least as a gunhand. Clean yourself up and maybe you can find yourself a job clerking in a general store or sweeping up a saloon somewhere. It just better be a long ways from here. If I ever see you again, I'll kill you. Remember that."

Cobb brought Beard's horse around saddled and ready to go, and Beard mounted up, groaning and whining. Slocum gave the horse a hard slap on the ass, and it bolted forward. Then Slocum and Cobb stood and watched as Beard rode out of sight on the road headed north away from Rat's Nest. "He won't be back," Cobb said. "That leaves eleven."

"Let's go on to town," said Slocum.

They rode cautiously into Rat's Nest and tied their horses in an alley behind the sheriff's office. It was an easy and secluded walk to the back door of the hotel where it might be possible to find at least a couple of Harman's men alone in their rooms. They had started to walk in that direction when Cobb put a hand on Slocum's shoulder. Slocum stopped and looked at Cobb. Cobb nodded toward the back door of the sheriff's office. Light could be seen under the door.

"What's that mean?" Slocum asked in a low voice.

"Looks like someone's in there," Cobb whispered. "I'd guess someone Harman put in. Do we go on to the hotel?"

Slocum pulled Cobb off a ways from the door. "Let's deal with this first," he said.

"That back door's most likely locked," said Cobb. "It don't hardly ever get used."

"We don't know who's in there," Slocum said, "nor how many of them. We need to find out. If you was to walk around there to the front, chances are you'd get spotted right quick. Everyone knows you. I'd best do it."

"All right," Cobb said, "but I'll go with you as far as the

corner of the building. I'll wait there in the shadows till I see what you're up to."

"Let's go," Slocum said, and he led the way around to the front corner of the sheriff's office. He looked up and down the street. There was a little traffic over in front of the Hi De Ho, but otherwise the street was almost deserted. He stepped out onto the board sidewalk and walked toward the front door of the sheriff's office and jail. When he reached the door he kept walking, but he glanced through the window and saw two men sitting and talking. A whiskey bottle sat on the desk between them. Past the window and out of their sight, Slocum stopped, turned, and raised two fingers. Cobb nodded. Slocum made a few quick gestures, and Cobb nodded again. Then he stepped out on the sidewalk and started walking. Slocum waited until Cobb was close to the door, then walked into him.

"Hey," Slocum shouted. "Watch where the hell you're going."

"You bumped into me," Cobb said.

Slocum shoved Cobb against the wall, and Cobb swung a right that glanced off Slocum's chin. The two men inside the office saw what was happening and stood up to watch through the window. Slocum drove a left into Cobb's belly, and Cobb wrapped his arms around Slocum, wrestling him back against the wall again. The men inside the office pressed their faces to the window to get a better look, but the two combatants were too far to one side. They moved to the door to open it, and just then Slocum flung Cobb against the door. The door flew open, and Cobb fell hard against one of the men. Both of them sprawled out on the floor.

"Hey," the other man said. "Take it back outside."

"Goddammit," said the man on the floor, struggling to get out from under Cobb and back up onto his feet. "You clumsy bastard."

Slocum stepped inside. "Let me at him," he snarled.

The man on his feet grabbed Slocum by a shoulder.

"Hold on there, pardner," he said, and Slocum swung a left hard into the man's jaw. He felt it crack. The man groaned and staggered back. He stood limply, holding his face in both hands. Slocum moved quickly to take the revolver out of the man's holster. He turned and leveled it at the other man, just getting to his feet.

The man stopped still. "What is this?" he said.

Cobb got to his feet and reached from behind the man to get his gun. "What the hell do we do with them now?" Cobb asked.

Slocum shrugged. "Put them in jail, I guess."

Cobb moved over to the nearest cell and swung the door open wide. "Come on, you two," he said.

The unhurt man turned to obey, and sudden recognition flashed over his face. "Eddie Cobb," he said. "You son of a bitch."

"Get in the cell," Cobb said.

"Hold it," Slocum said, stepping over in front of the man. He looked down at the holster hanging on the man's left hip. "A leftie, huh?" Slocum said.

The man looked puzzled. "So what?" he said.

Slocum reached out, grabbed the man's left-hand index finger, and with a quick twist snapped it. The man yowled in pain. Slocum shoved him toward the cell. Then he went back for the other one who was still sagging and holding his face. "I don't think this one'll be doing much fighting for a spell," he said, "but I don't like taking chances." He grabbed the right index finger of that one and jerked it back. The bone broke with a loud crack, and the man hollered, but the movement of his jaw hurt even more. He resorted to whimpering as Slocum pushed him into the cell with the other man. Cobb shut the door and locked it.

"Get the keys," said Slocum, "and let's take all the guns and ammunition out of here."

"You goddamn dirty bastards," said the left-handed man. "Harman'll get you for this."

"He'll have to do it with only nine men," said Cobb, "and that's counting him."

"Let's go," said Slocum.

Loaded up with rifles, six-guns, boxes of ammunition, and the big key ring, Slocum and Cobb went out the back door of the sheriff's office and moved quickly over to their horses. Slocum unraveled a length of lariat off his saddle. He strung the extra six-guns onto the rope by poking its end through their trigger guards, then lapped the rope several times around the rifles to make a bundle. He tied the bundle behind his saddle. He and Cobb stuffed the boxes of ammunition into their saddlebags. From inside the jail, a voice started to howl out for help.

"What now?" Cobb asked.

"Let's not push our luck," said Slocum. "Let's just get the hell out of here." They mounted up and started to ride back out of town. A few miles down the road, Eddie Cobb tossed the key ring into some bushes.

Back at the ranch, they found Joiner, Bobby, Myrtle, and Julia waiting anxiously for their return. "God, we're glad to see you back here safe," Joiner said.

"Tell us what happened," said Myrtle.

"We only got nine of them to worry about now," Cobb said, in partial answer.

Slocum walked over to the big table and sat down. "Let's sit here and talk about it over a glass of whiskey," he said. Myrtle hurried for the bottle while Julia got out six glasses and put them on the table. Everyone sat down to a glass except Joiner. He hesitated.

"Sit down, Chuckie," said Slocum.

"But you said—"

"I know what I said," Slocum declared. "Right now I'm asking you to join us."

Joiner sat down as Myrtle handed the bottle to Slocum. He poured himself a glassful and passed the bottle to Eddie Cobb. Soon it had gone all the way around the table. Only then did Slocum raise his glass. "Pardners," he said, "for the first time since we got ourselves into this, it looks like we got a chance to win it." Then they all drank.

"All right," Myrtle said, "you going to tell us now?"

"Go on ahead," Slocum said to Cobb.

"Well," Cobb said, "first thing, we stopped off at old Harvey Beard's house, 'cause, you know, he lives outside of town all by his lonesome. Ole Slocum here broke his arm, and we sent him on his way north. We went on into town then, thinking we'd try to sneak up on some of them in their hotel rooms, but instead we seen that they had a light on in the sheriff's office. We found two of them in there, and we busted their trigger fingers and locked them up in a cell. We took all the guns and ammunition that was in the office and decided that we'd call it a night. So we trimmed them down from twelve to nine and didn't even have to kill no one."

"I'll be damned," Joiner said.

"So what's our next move?" Myrtle said.

"That's a damn good question," Slocum said. "If we sit out here waiting for Harman to make the next move, he might just send out of town for more gunhands. I don't think we can afford to give him time for that. If we try to go back to town the way we did tonight, we might run into a little more trouble. He'll be expecting it now. Likely they'll all hang together somewhere. Probably in the Hi De Ho, and we won't get to pick them off one or two at a time. The only other thing I can think of is to try to call them out for a face-off. All of them and all of us right out in the open. And I don't think we can do that by just riding in there ready for a fight. Like I said before, we'd look like a gang of outlaws pulling a raid. We don't want to put folks on their side."

"So what do we do?" Joiner said.

"We need to get folks on our side before we call Harman and his bunch out," Slocum said.

"How are we going to do that?" Myrtle asked.

"How do the other ranchers around here feel about Harman?" Slocum said.

"About the way we do," Myrtle said.

"They just haven't been able to do anything about him," Julia added. "They're either afraid or—whatever. I don't know."

"Up until Harman's bunch killed Bud," Cobb said, "they came to the law with their complaints and suspicions. But they never had no proof, and Bud always said we have to have proof. We have to do things within the law. I guess most folks around here was just hoping that one of these days Bud would come up with some kind of evidence against Harman."

"Can you all get a bunch of people together for a meeting?" Slocum asked. "Right here?"

The others all looked at each other, and finally Myrtle answered. "Yeah," she said. "I think so. Mort Hindman would come, and Bailey and—and—Harris."

"Brick Thurman," said Julia. "He'll come."

"I can think of another half dozen at least," said Cobb. "Hell, any of the honest folks around these parts would, I believe."

"All right," Slocum said. "Here's the way I see it. We get all these folks over here, and let Chuckie tell them his story about what Harman done to him, why he's been gone for two years, how Harman got his hands on this ranch, the whole story, then wind it up with a showing of the evidence that proves that Harman was behind all the rustling all this time. That should get them convinced and get them on our side. Right?"

"Sure it will," said Joiner.

"I think so," Cobb agreed. "Like I said before, they all been just waiting for someone to come up with proof against Harman and his bunch."

"Okay," Slocum said. "So we get them convinced, get them on our side, then we pop this one on them. The sheriff's been killed, now Joe Short's dead too, and even if he wasn't dead, he was with Harman. The only legitimate law left here is Eddie Cobb, and he's here with us. With all that fresh information in their heads, we tell them that we're going to town to clean Harman and them out once and for all. We tell them to spread the word to all the decent folks that we're in the right on this deal, and we got the law with us, and to stay out of the way when it happens. What do you say?"

"Let's do it," said Joiner.

"I agree," Cobb said.

"It sounds good to me," said Myrtle.

"Me too," Julia agreed.

"Then, by God," said Slocum, "let's drink to it."

They all lifted their glasses together. Slocum drained his glass and stood up. "On that," he said, "I think I'll turn in. I don't think we'll have any visitors tonight, but just to be safe, we ought to keep a watch."

"I'll watch." Bobby said. "I ain't done no good today yet. Reckon it's my turn."

As Slocum headed for the bedroom, Myrtle watched him greedily. Eddie Cobb headed for the couch in the big room, and Joiner and Julia unashamedly headed up the stairs together.

9

Slocum had pulled off his shirt and his boots. He was unfastening his jeans when the door to his room opened. He looked over his shoulder to see Myrtle. She stood there a moment, the door still partially open, and she was a silhouette against the light in the other room. "You mind if I come in?" she asked.

"Shut the door and come on," he said.

She stepped in and turned to shut the door and latch it. "Do you mind some company?" she said. "How's your shoulder?"

"Lady," he said, moving to the lamp on the table, "everything on me is working just fine." He struck a match and lit the lamp, then turned the flame down low.

"You want a light on?" she asked.

"You've seen me," he said. "Now I get to see you."

"All right," she said. She sat in a chair and pulled off her boots. Then she stood and unfastened her jeans. Slocum watched her in eager anticipation as she slowly lowered her jeans to reveal shapely legs. Her britches down on the floor, she pulled first one bare foot, then the other loose from the rumpled denim and kicked the jeans aside. She crossed her arms, taking hold of the tail of her shirt, and pulled it up over her head. Then she shook her head to get her hair back out of her face. She stood there in glorious nakedness, and Slocum was thrilled.

His eyes traveled from her bare feet up her long and lovely legs to the dark bush that hid damp treasures. Her hips were wide and smooth, and her waist was narrow. Her belly was flat and firm, and further up a bountiful pair of breasts thrust themselves eagerly toward him, their nipples large and hard and begging to be licked and sucked. She bent over to pick up her shirt and jeans, then turned to drop them on the chair behind her, but really, she turned to show him her ample ass. Slocum felt the tool between his legs begin to stiffen and push itself against his jeans. He shoved them down and stepped out of them as she moved toward him, her mouth slightly open, her lips wet and inviting.

She stepped up close, put her arms around his shoulders, and pressed her whole nakedness against his. Her tits were mashed against his chest, and his cock throbbed against her belly. She tilted her head back as he leaned forward to place his lips on hers, and their tongues darted into each other's mouths and roamed and probed. Slocum put his hands on her head and ran his fingers deep into her thick blond hair, pulling her face harder against his own. Her hands slid down his back to first grip his ass cheeks, then move around to grasp his stiff rod and full balls. His cock jumped in her hand.

They relaxed the kiss and backed off slightly from one another, feeling each other's hot breath against their faces. Slocum stepped back slightly and sat down on the edge of the bed. He put his hands on her slender waist and turned her around, then pulled her back toward him. She got the idea quickly, arched her back, thrust her ass at him, then lowered herself to sit on his cock, taking its full length up into her ready, wet cunt. She sat down hard on him with all her weight, and she gasped out loud at the thrill of it.

Slocum sucked in a deep breath, held it a moment, then expelled it in a long sigh. God, she was smooth and silky inside, and the muscles of her living cunt began to squeeze his rod up and down its length. She started to rock on his thighs, shoving her ass back against his belly and drawing it forward again, slowly back and forth, then a little faster and harder. It was wonderful, but Slocum was inactive. He was again the recipient of her delights. This time he wanted a more active role to play. He lifted her slightly off his lap, then a little higher, until only the head of his cock was still inside her pussy. Then he lowered her again. She picked up on that idea and bounced up and down on him, splashing her juices on his thighs with a lovely squishing sound.

As she rose again, he lifted her all the way off. His wet cock slapped back against his belly as it was suddenly released from her wet cavern of delight. He stood up and guided her to the bed, putting her on her back. She smiled at him and spread her legs wide apart. He crawled between them, and she reached for the sticky, wet shaft to guide it back into her pleasure hole. Slocum drove it all the way in, and she gasped and lifted her legs, thrusting upward with her own hips, grinding against him. Then they were still for a moment, savoring the feel of the deep penetration. The walls of her cunt squeezed him up and down, and his cock throbbed inside her.

Then he started to thrust, slowly at first, then faster and harder, pounding against her pelvis, his rod driving deep and hard into her cunt, his heavy balls slapping against her ass. Her breathing turned to fast, breathy panting, and with each thrust her lips let out a small whimper. "Uh, uh, uh."

Slocum slowed his pace and continued his thrusts more slowly. He wasn't ready to unload in this lovely cunt—not just yet. Then he pulled out again and straightened himself up on his knees there between her wide-spread legs. He looked down at the wet and gleaming pussy there before him. "Turn over," he said.

She flopped quickly over onto her belly, then crawled up on her knees, her round, tight ass shoving itself up towards him. He grasped his rod and poked it back into her luscious cunt and resumed pounding his flesh against hers. "Ah," she cried. "Oh, God. Fuck me, John. Fuck me hard." He slammed his pelvis against her lovely ass over and over again, driving his rod deep into her willing cunt. Juice ran down the inside of her thighs and down the length of his rod and onto his balls.

Suddenly Slocum felt the building surge inside him. It was as if he would explode from deep down inside his balls with the tremendous pressure that had developed there. He pounded harder and faster, and then it came. He shot a load deep inside her cunt, and then another and another. He kept thrusting, beating his body against hers, feeling more release with each spurt, and then finally it was over. He stayed inside her, breathing deeply, not moving. At last she broke the silence. "God," she said, "you flooded me. That was wonderful."

He backed out, turned, and fell back onto the bed there beside her. His wet cock, now limp, lay back on his belly. She turned to kiss him on the lips, and her hand roamed down his chest and belly to the wet and sticky cock. She gripped it in her hand and slid her fingers up and down its length. Finally she moved away, got out of bed, and walked to the table across the room. She picked up a towel there, dipped it into the water bowl, wrung it out, and went back to the bed. Crawling up beside him, she began to wash the come juices off his cock and balls and belly and thighs.

"I knew you'd be a great lover, John," she said. "I've just been dying for this night."

"I've been pretty anxious for it myself," he said.

She laid the wet towel on the bedside table and snuggled up against him, her head on his chest. One hand still held his cock. "Um," she said. "I love it." She raised her head and kissed him tenderly on the lips, and he put an arm around her and held her close. She crawled on top of him, and the feel of the whole length of her nakedness against him was as if he had died and gone to some kind of heaven. Just then, his cock surprised him by starting to stir again.

It surprised Myrtle too as she felt it rise up between her legs.

John," she said, "what a surprise."

"Yes," he said, and wrapped his arms around her and rolled them over, placing himself on top again. She reached down with both her hands and guided his cock back into the depths of her still-juicy cunt, and they made quiet love for a long time. At last, Slocum felt the buildup inside his balls again, and for a short time he pumped hard and fast and then the release came suddenly. He rolled off to her side.

"That was lovely," she said, and kissed him tenderly. Again she washed him, and they lay side by side quietly until they both slept.

Slocum slept hard. It was the morning sun coming in through the window that woke him up at last. He opened his eyes to see a vision of glorious womanhood sitting beside him on the bed, looking down at him with a slight smile on her face. "You were sleeping so well," Myrtle said. "I didn't want to wake you."

He reached up to put a hand on her shoulder.

"You want some coffee?" she asked him.

"No," he said. "Not yet. I want you."

He pulled her toward him for a kiss, and she reached for his cock. It reacted quickly, stiffening to her touch. Slocum thought that he had taken so much pleasure from her body the night before, it was time to give her as much as he could. He pulled her over on top, and she eased herself down on his rod. She started to rock gently.

Then she rocked faster and faster, and then she began to tremble, and then her body jerked with the intense pleasure that sent waves of shock through her body. She kept going, and the surge of pleasure intensified. She gasped and moaned. "Oh, God," she said. "Oh, God." She rocked harder, almost viciously, as if she would tear the cock right off his body with her rocking and thrusting, and the slimy wetness that developed between their two bodies gave her a wonderful surface on which to thrust. Her climax continued as she kept up the pace.

It built in intensity until her moans grew louder, and Slocum was sure that everyone in the house could hear her. He didn't care. It was wonderful what was happening to Myrtle. He could tell that she was enjoying the greatest pleasure a woman could experience. She was having one long orgasm that just wouldn't quit, and she wouldn't let it quit. She kept rocking and thrusting, sliding on his pelvis, jerking his rod back and forth with her motions, fucking him as hard as she could fuck, as if her life and everything in the whole world depended on the fury of this one magnificent fuck.

Then, at last, she threw her head back and heaved an audible sigh. "Ah," she said, "Oh, God, John, I can't stand it any longer. Any more would kill me. I know it would." She reached around behind herself, down below her own ass and farther, until she found his balls, and she gripped them hard. Slocum thrust upward with a start. He thrust again and his cock gushed forth a massive load into her already soppy cunt. A mixture of both their body juices ran down Slocum's balls and her hand, which still held them tight.

She cleaned them off once again, and they got out of bed and into their clothes. Myrtle walked to the door and opened it. She hesitated there, and Slocum stepped up behind her. Looking over her shoulder, he saw what she had seen. The others were sitting at the big table, and all eyes were looking at them, all faces wearing knowing expressions. "Well, hell," Slocum said, his voice low in her ear, "let's go on and get ourselves some coffee and breakfast."

Myrtle, with a sudden resolve, tossed her head and walked proudly into the main room.

"I am in a position," she said out loud for all to hear, "to announce without any doubt that John Slocum is fully recovered from his wound."

• • •

Julia had already laid out a sumptuous breakfast. When Slocum and Myrtle approached the table, she stood up. "Both of you sit down," she said. "I'll serve you. I doubt if either one of you has any strength left."

Joiner guffawed. "I guess she said it right."

Slocum pulled out a chair for Myrtle to sit in, then seated himself beside her. "Chuckie boy," he said, "we ain't made no comments about your activities upstairs. What happens behind closed bedroom doors ain't no one else's business."

Bobby and Eddie both looked down into their plates. Both their faces were flushed. Slocum thought that those two men were most likely suffering mightily, knowing what was going on in two bedrooms of the big house at night. He decided that something ought to be done about that. If it could be done without endangering them all.

Julia brought out coffee for Slocum and Myrtle, then went back into the kitchen for their plates. She came back out and put plates before them. Then the platters of eggs, potatoes, bacon, and biscuits and the bowl of gravy were all passed to them. Slocum thought that he would be able to eat until all the food was gone from all the platters, but he was a little surprised when Myrtle dished herself out generous second helpings of everything. Finished with their meals at last, they all sat around the table having one more cup of coffee.

"Today's the day for setting up our big meeting," Slocum said. "Who's going to spread the word?"

"It has to be some of us," Joiner said. "You're a stranger to everyone around here."

"I'll stay and keep an eye on things here," Slocum said.

"I ought to go," Cobb said. "I think folks trust me, and I think they'll accept the authority of my badge."

"That's good," Slocum said. "How many of them can you get around to in just one day?"

"I think I can get to most of them," Cobb said. "Course, ole Brick Thurman's way on east of here. I wouldn't be able to get to him the same day, not and get back here."

"I'll go see Brick," Joiner said. "He's an old friend. No matter what kind of lies Harman has spread about me, Brick will trust me. He'll believe what I say."

"I'll ride along with you," Julia said. "If I have to stay in the house much longer I'll go crazy. I feel almost like we're in jail here."

Joiner looked at Slocum. "You think that'd be all right?" he asked. "For Julia to ride along?"

"Just be careful," Slocum said. "Keep your eyes open. Don't let any of Harman's bunch see you. Likely, after what's happened to them, they'll be hanging together in Rat's Nest. Even so, be careful. That goes for you too, Eddie."

"Don't worry," Cobb said. "I'll be watching in every direction all at the same time. I ain't anxious to get myself filled full of lead."

"All right," Slocum said. "How soon can we get this meeting called for?"

"Tomorrow morning," said Cobb. "By the time I get the word spread all over out this direction, most of the day will be gone. Best I can do is ask folks to gather up here in the morning."

"That makes sense to me," said Joiner.

"Tomorrow morning then," Slocum said. "You all best get going then. Me and Bobby and Myrtle will keep our eyes on things here while you're gone."

The women packed some trail food for Eddie Cobb and for Joiner and Julia. Then each of the riders selected a revolver and a rifle. They also packed plenty of ammunition just in case. They saddled three of the best horses, and then rode off together down the lane. Later, out on the road, they would part company, Cobb going one way, Joiner and Julia the other. Slocum, Bobby, and Myrtle stood on the porch watching them until they were out of sight. Slocum found himself wishing that he had some chore to send Bobby on too, so that he could be alone with Myrtle. He knew that was a foolish thought. Alone with Myrtle, he would have to stay alert in case of a sneak attack from Harman's men.

He thought about taking Myrtle back to bed and letting Bobby stand watch, but that thought made him feel guilty. He wouldn't really be able to enjoy himself, knowing that for his own selfish pleasure he was letting someone else do the work, someone who was without his own woman and therefore frustrated. It just wouldn't feel right. Even so, Slocum was lusting for more adventures with the naked loveliness of Myrtle. Damn, but she was good. He had never had anyone like her. Had never known anyone like her.

She could cook and she could shoot. She was cool under fire and under pressure. Nothing ruffled her. Her company was pleasant, and her lovemaking was out of this world. Slocum found himself wondering if he could actually settle down after all these years. If there had ever been a woman who could make him do it, Myrtle was the one. They would get Joiner his ranch back, and Slocum was sure that he would be able to stay on there for as long as he might want to. He could make a home there, a home for himself and . . . He tried to stop himself from thinking in that direction. It frightened him, and that surprised him.

But he . . . He stopped himself again. He had almost said, albeit only in his mind, had almost said that he loved her. He refused to allow himself to have that thought, or at least to fully express it. He did have strong feelings for her, he allowed his brain to say. He could live with her. He could make a home with her. Or could he? Would it work? And would it be worth the pain he would ultimately cause himself and her to try it out for a while, only to have to abandon it later?

He had a hell of a dilemma, and he asked himself if it was worth it, for all of the intense pleasure they had given one another, to wind up with this problem. He thought about the events of last night and early this morning. He tried to recall the beauty of her naked body, the feel of that flesh against his own, the sensations of—Hell, yes, he told himself. It had damn sure been worth it. The times he had spent with her, the things they done together, it was all worth anything that could possibly happen to him. It was worth having taken the slug in his shoulder, for if that had not happened to him, he would have ignored Joiner's pleas for his help and ridden on west alone.

What a thought. He was actually grateful to whichever of Harman's gunnies had drilled him. The man had brought him to all the wonder of Myrtle's pleasure house. He would have to try to figure out which one of the bastards had dry-gulched him, find the right grave, and go put a flower on it or something. Myrtle and her joyous and wonderful love-making were well worth a bullet, were worth fighting a whole army alone, were worth fighting a panther bare-handed. She was worth whole worlds, and he sure had a lot of things to think about.

Slocum settled down. He tried to picture himself sitting comfortably before a roaring fire, his slippered feet propped up on a plush hassock. He saw himself behind a counter in a general store counting out change for a gray-haired woman who had just purchased a bolt of cloth. Then he saw himself standing in a field, a hoe in his hands, wearing a pair of loose-fitting denim overalls, with a straw hat on his head. The sun was beating down from overhead, and he was mopping his forehead with a red bandanna.

And then a final image flashed into his mind. He saw himself standing alone in a room, a howling infant nestled in each of his arms. Twins. With a sense of horror and impending doom, he shook the frightening images out of his head. God, he thought. That was a close call. But just when he thought that he had cleared his head, the other images returned to haunt him, the more pleasant ones, the images of the sleek, delightful body, the remembrances of the deep and wonderful pleasures it had given him.

10

Eddie Cobb made it to the first ranch on his list about mid-morning. He turned his horse into the lane that led to the ranch house, a modest frame home. He knew that Mort Hindman had lived alone since the loss of his wife ten years back. Lately Mort had fallen on hard times. Losses from the rustlers had depleted his herd. He'd been forced to let all his hands go except for old Hiram McCulley, and the two old men were just barely scraping together a living for themselves on the place. It was a shame. The Hindman Ranch had once been a thriving place. As Cobb approached the front of the house, he was greeted by a harsh voice.

"Hold it right there, stranger."

Cobb stopped his horse and lifted his hands. He looked toward the voice, and there, behind a long-barreled shotgun poking around the corner of the house, was old Hiram. "Hiram," Cobb said, "lower your gun, old-timer." Hiram McCulley squinted. "Eddie Cobb," he said, "that you?"

"Yeah," Cobb said. "It's me. Will you lower that gun and let me step down?"

"Sure, sure," said McCulley. "I didn't rekernize you, Eddie. Climb on down and come in the house. Mort's going to be real glad to see you. Yes, sir. We don't get many

visitors out here, you know. Come on in. Come in, and I'll
fetch you a cup of coffee."

Cobb swung down out of the saddle and followed
McCulley into the house. As he stepped through the door,
McCulley called out, "Mort. Mort, come on out here. We
got us some company, Mort. Eddie Cobb's here."

A door to a bedroom opened, and Mort Hindman poked
his head out. "Eddie?" he said. "Eddie, welcome. Get some
coffee, Hiram."

"What do you think I'm doing?" McCulley said.

"Sit down," said Hindman. He indicated a chair to Cobb,
and Cobb sat. Hindman sat in a chair facing him. McCulley
brought two cups of coffee and handed one to each of the
other two men. He went back to get one for himself. Cobb
tried not to be too obvious about taking in the shabby sur-
roundings. The place sure had gone down since Mrs. Hindman's death. It was a sad sight to Cobb.

"Thanks," he said to McCulley. He took a sip of the hot
coffee. It was old. He could tell. McCulley had likely
brewed it early that morning, and the pot had never been
finished. "Good coffee," he said. "How've you all been out
here?"

"We're making out," Hindman said. He sipped his coffee. "Tastes like shit, Hiram," he said.

"You're lucky to have it," said McCulley. "Enjoy it.
We're damn near out."

"You all heard the news from town?" Cobb asked.

"Ain't been to town in—"

"Six months," said McCulley, finishing Hindman's sen-
tence for him. "And ain't had no visitors since—"

"Three months ago," Hindman said, "when that drummer
come by." He laughed, and McCulley joined in the laughter. "Tried to sell me a gadget to peel apples with," Hindman added. The two old men laughed harder. "Ain't seen
an apple in—"

"Nigh onto six years," said McCulley.

Cobb let their laughter die down, and then he said, "Let

me tell you what's been happening. You know, about two years ago, Clyde Harman got Charlie Joiner accused of rustling? Charlie damn near got lynched over it."

"I remember that," Hindman said. "Bunch of bullshit. Charlie ain't no rustler. I knowed his daddy back in the old days."

"I agree with that," Cobb said. "Anyhow, Charlie got loose and left the country. Went down south of the border. Well, he's back, and he's brought proof that the rustling was done by Harman."

"Hot damn," said McCulley, jumping up from his chair. "I knowed it. I knowed it all along. That two-bit slimy dog-fucking son of a bitch Harman. Hot damn. I knowed it."

"Sit down and shut up, Hiram," Hindman said. Then, to Cobb, he said "What else?"

"Well, Charlie brought another fellow with him," Cobb said. "Man called Slocum. And when Charlie and Slocum sneaked back on Charlie's ranch to take it over, Bobby Hale was there. Remember Bobby?"

"I know Bobby," said Hindman. "Go on."

"Well, Bobby tossed in with Charlie," said Cobb, "and they got two women with them. Charlie's old gal, Julia, and Myrtle Bingham. Both gals can shoot too. Anyhow, when Bud Coleman found out about Charlie's evidence on Harman, he went to arrest Harman, and Harman or some of his men killed Bud."

"Aw," said Hindman. "Aw, I'm sorry to hear that. Bud was a good man. Aw, hell."

"That slimy dog bastard Harman," said McCulley.

"The way it's shook down," Cobb said, "is that I been out at the ranch with Joiner and them others, and we're fixing to have us a showdown in Rat's Nest. We aim to ride in there and call out Harman and his whole crew, but we want you and all the other decent folks around here to know what's going on. We want you to know that I'm still a deputy, and so the law is in on this, and we want you to know that we got proof on Harman. I come to ask you to be over at Charlie's ranch in the morning for a meeting to talk about all this and inform everyone what's going on. Can you be there?"

"Damn straight we'll be there," McCulley said.

"You bet," said Hindman. "We'll come, and if you need extra guns when you go to have the showdown, you can count on us for that too."

"Well," Cobb said, "we'll see about that later. Just be at the ranch in the morning. We'll talk more then. And thanks. I got to be going to spread the word around some more."

As Cobb headed for the door, Hindman stood up. "We'll help you out with that too," he said. "Hiram, go saddle our horses. You just tell us where to go, Eddie. We'll help you gather them up."

At the Bailey place, Cobb also met with approval and instant agreement. He got away as fast as he could and headed for Harris's ranch. Hindman and McCulley were headed into an area that he hadn't even planned to visit. He was feeling good. They should have a sizable gathering at Charlie Joiner's ranch in the morning.

At about that same time, Charlie Joiner and Julia rode side by side up to the front of Brick Thurman's house. Thurman stepped out the door, having heard the sound of approaching riders. "Charlie," he said. "Goddamn. It's good to see you, boy. I heard you was back in these parts."

"You hear I got my ranch back?" Joiner asked.

"I heard that too," said Thurman. "Come on down, and let's have us a drink together."

Joiner dismounted and wrapped his horse's reins around the hitching rail. He did the same with Julia's horse and helped her down off its back. Thurman had walked up close to him by then, and the two men shook hands heartily. Joiner thought of Slocum's caution to him about drinking, and he considered his own weakness. "I'll settle for coffee just now, Brick," he said. "You know Julia here?"

"Sure," Thurman said. "I remember her. Welcome, Julia. I'm sure glad to see you both, but I got a feeling you come for more than just a friendly visit. Come on in the house, and I'll get us some coffee."

Joiner and Julia followed Thurman into the house, where Mrs. Thurman met them with a friendly smile. "Mama," said Thurman, "you remember Charlie here and his gal, Julia."

"Why, yes," said Mrs. Thurman. "How do you do?"

"Just fine, ma'am," Joiner said.

"I offered them a cup of coffee," Thurman said.

"I'll fetch it," said Mrs. Joiner, and she turned to head for the kitchen. Julia followed her. "I'll help you," she said. "Oh, it ain't no bother," said Mrs. Thurman, but Julia followed her just the same.

"Sit down," Thurman said to Joiner, and the two men sat.

"Where you been all this time, Charlie?" Thurman said. "Mexico?"

"You guessed it," said Joiner. "Harman had me pegged for a rustler. I never was, but—"

"Hell, I know that," Thurman said.

"Anyhow, he had me pegged that way, and I had to get out for a while," Joiner said. The two women came out of the kitchen and served coffee around. "But I wasn't just hiding down there," Joiner went on. "I was looking out for them stolen cows that I figured was being sold down there. Finally I got lucky. It was Harman's men, all right. I got some papers down there that prove it, and that's when I decided to come on back. Picked up a new partner along the way too. His name's John Slocum."

"Slocum?" said Thurman, stroking his chin. "Seems like I heard that name somewhere. Gunfighter?"

"Well," Joiner said, "he's handy enough with his guns. He saved my life down in Mexico. He's out at the ranch right now with Myrtle Bingham and Bobby Hale. I come out here to see you, and Eddie Cobb's gone out west to round up the other ranchers out that way. We want you all to come to a meeting at my place in the morning."

"Well, sure, Charlie," Thurman said. "But what for? What are we meeting about?"

"It's like this, Brick," Joiner said. "We've already cut down Harman's force to nine men. That counts Harman himself. I've got the proof that Harman's been the rustler all along, and we've got Eddie Cobb with us. Harman had Bud Coleman killed, you know, and Joe Short was in cahoots with him. That leaves just Eddie to represent the law, and Eddie's with us.

"Well, we don't want to ride into town and just call Harman and his gang out for a showdown without all you folks know what's going on and how come we're doing it. We want everyone to know that we got the law on our side. And we got right on our side. But we can't just ask Eddie to go arrest them. That's what Bud tried to do, and they just killed him. Just like that. So we just want everyone around to know what the deal is. That's all. We ain't asking no one to get into the fight with us."

"We'll be at your meeting in the morning," Thurman said. "Me and Mama. I'll bring along some of the boys too."

"Thanks, Brick," said Joiner. "It'll mean a lot having you there."

"Why don't you two stay the night with us?" Mrs. Thurman said. "We can all ride back over there together in the morning."

"Thank you," Joiner said, "but I reckon we'd better head on back. If we don't show up, Slocum and the rest might get to worrying about us."

They were mounted up and back on the road, moving along at a leisurely pace. "It's looking good, Charlie," Julia said. "With Brick Thurman backing us up, no one'll doubt our story. Everyone will know we're in the right."

"I don't guess there's much worry about that," Joiner

said. "This was a good idea that John had. Course, all his ideas are good ones. I don't know where I'd be right now without him."

They rode on a little farther, and then they saw four riders coming toward them. The riders were moving casually, and they did not look familiar to either Joiner or Julia. "Could be just strangers riding through," Julia said.

"Could be," said Joiner, "but be careful, just in case." He rested the palm of his right hand on the butt of his revolver. They rode closer.

"It's four Mexicans," Julia said. "Harman's got no Mexicans in his gang."

"Unless he's been recruiting new guns already," Joiner said. "We better hold up here." He moved off to the side of the road, and Julia moved off to the other side. They waited for the four Mexican riders to approach. A little nearer, one of the riders spoke up. *"Buenos dias,"* he said. "Is it far to the next town?"

"The way you're headed," Joiner said, "it's a couple of days."

"Is there a nearer town, Señor," the man asked, "if we choose another way?"

"Back toward the border," Joiner said, "there's a little place called Rat's Nest. It ain't far."

"Gracias, Señor," the Mexican said. "We have already come through there. I guess we'll ride for two more days to find the other town."

The four riders tipped their sombreros and rode on. Joiner and Julia watched them over their shoulders for a moment. Then, convinced that the four were actually what they seemed, four strangers riding through, they faced forward again and urged their mounts on. All of a sudden, shots were fired. Joiner looked back, and the four Mexicans had turned and were shooting at them. He jerked the Winchester out of the scabbard at his horse's side and cranked a shell into the chamber. Just then a bullet smacked into his horse. It screamed in pain, reared, and dumped Joiner onto the ground. He lost his rifle as he fell. The wounded horse stamped and milled about in the road.

"Run, Julia. Run," Joiner yelled.

"I won't leave you," she said, pulling the rifle from her own scabbard. She jacked a shell into the chamber.

"Julia," Joiner said. "Get out of here. Go get Slocum."

She turned her horse and rode as hard as she could. Joiner looked at the Mexicans, now close to him again, and he raised his hands. "I got no money, *compadres,*" he said. "I got nothing but a couple of guns. You're welcome to them."

"We don't need your guns, amigo," said the spokeman of the group, "but we will take them away from you. We don't want you to try nothing foolish." One of the riders dismounted and took Joiner's six-gun and his rifle "Now get up on your feet," the spokesman said.

Joiner stood up. "What's this all about?" he asked:

"You don't know me, Señor?" the man asked. "You don't recognize me or my friends? You have such a short memory, gringo. Of course, you saw us only twice. The first time it was dark. The second time we were clear across the river from each other. And then too, we were wearing uniforms those times. Well, at least part of the time. Do you remember us now, Señor?"

By the time he had finished his little speech, the man had ridden up close to Joiner. He slipped his foot out of the stirrup and swung it hard, giving Joiner a hard but glancing blow to the side of the head. Joiner spun around and fell hard.

"Get up, Señor," the man said. "We can't leave you here like this. Lying helpless, alone and unarmed, with no horse out in the middle of nowhere. Get up on your feet."

Joiner struggled up and rubbed the side of his head. "I got a horse," he said.

"Oh, no, amigo," the rider said. "You don't got no horse. We are taking your horse."

"Look," Joiner said. "Okay. I know who you are now.

You're those *rurales* that chased us out of Mexico. But we didn't do nothing illegal down there. We run off from you because we just didn't want to get tangled up in no investigation. We had things to get to up here. You go back down there and ask Pee-dro in that cantina. That hombre was fixing to back shoot me. Pee-dro can tell you that."

"Is that right, hombre?" the rurale said. "I don't care about that stinking dead gringo no more. You and your amigo pulled your guns on us. You and your amigo made us take off our clothes and walk to the river. You and your fucking amigo embarrassed us, and we don't want to let you get away with that."

He made a wild gesture with his right arm, and another of the *rurales* swung a lariat, tossing a loop around Joiner. He jerked it tight before Joiner could react.

"Get his *caballo,* Pepe," the leader said, and the man called Pepe rode over to take the reins of Joiner's horse.

"Wait a minute," Joiner said. "Whatever you think about what happened down there, you got no authority in Texas."

"Authority?" said the *rurale* leader. "What authority? Do you see uniforms? Do you see badges? Fuck you, and fuck authority. You insulted us. You and your fucking amigo. We don't like to be insulted, hombre."

"You mean to kill me for making you take a hike without your uniforms on?" Joiner said.

"We might kill you," the man said. "We might peel off some of your white skin. We don't know yet just what we'll do with you, but you won't like it, hombre. You can be sure of that. And we won't kill you before your fucking amigo comes to save you. Then we'll get him too."

"He's long gone," Joiner said.

"Oh, yeah? We'll see about that, gringo. We'll see. Why do you think we let the pretty little gringa ride away so easy? We could have stopped her. We could have killed her. We could have taken her and fucked her a few times. Maybe we'll do that later. Who knows? But we let her go so she could go to your fucking amigo for help. You stupid gringos. Enough talking. Let's go."

He turned his horse and kicked it hard into a run. The others followed him, one leading Joiner's horse, another pulling Joiner along at the end of his lariat. Joiner ran as hard as he could to keep up, but soon he was jerked off his feet. He landed hard on his belly, then felt himself being dragged across the rough land, bouncing, bumping, twisting at the end of the rope, and then, mercifully, everything went black.

11

Bobby rushed to meet Julia as she came pounding up to the house, her horse sweating and panting. It was obvious that something was wrong. She wouldn't otherwise have so mistreated a horse. He grabbed the reins to settle the poor animal down, and Julia swung down off its back fast. Just then Slocum came out of the house, followed closely by Myrtle. Julia ran toward Slocum, almost collapsing against his chest. "What's happened?" he asked.

"Oh, John," she said. "We've got to hurry."

"All right, but first tell me what's wrong. Where's Chuck?"

"They've got him," Julia said. "Four of them. I wanted to stay and help him, but he told me to ride out. Oh, come on. They might have already killed him. We've got to go. Please."

"I'll go," Slocum said. "You just tell me where to go, and tell me what happened. Who's got him?"

"We were coming back from Mr. Thurman's ranch," Julia said, "and we met four men on the road. We were cautious, but then, we didn't recognize them. They were strangers. Mexicans. We rode past each other. We thought they'd gone on their way. Suddenly they turned and rode hard at us. They knocked Charlie off his horse, and he told me to run. I have to go back with you, John. I can't tell you exactly where it happened, but I can show you."

"We'll all go," Myrtle said.

"No, we won't," said Slocum. "If they're some new men Harman got, that might be his plan. Get us all away from the ranch at the same time. Besides, what would Eddie think if he was to get back and find no one here? No. Julia can take me to where it happened, and I'll take it from there. Bobby, will you saddle up my horse and a fresh one for Julia?"

"Sure," Bobby said.

He headed for the corral, leading Julia's spent horse, and Slocum went back inside. He got his hat, strapped on his gunbelt, and picked up his Winchester. He grabbed an extra box of .45 shells, then glanced at Julia, who had followed him into the house. "Are you ready?" he said.

"Yes," she said. "We've got to hurry."

Myrtle grabbed Slocum around his shoulders with both her arms. "Be careful, John," she said. "We can't afford to lose both of you."

"If we ain't too late, I mean to see that we don't lose no one."

He gave Myrtle a quick kiss and broke free of her embrace. "Let's go, Julia," he said. The two of them hurried outside, where Bobby had already led the two horses up to the porch. He helped Julia up onto the back of her mount, as Slocum swung up into the saddle on top of his big Appaloosa. "Lead the way," he said, "but don't ride as hard as you come in. We don't want to wear these horses out before we get there."

It was all Julia could do to hold back, but she knew that Slocum was right about the horses. They rode side by side down the lane and onto the road, where Julia turned east. Slocum followed along, then moved back up beside her. "Try not to worry too much," he said. "If they didn't shoot him down right away, likely they don't mean to. Not till they draw us out."

"What do you mean?" she said.

"It's my guess that they grabbed him hoping to draw the rest of us away from the ranch," Slocum said. "They'll probably keep him alive long enough to do that. Well, their scheme worked—partly. It drawed me and you. For the rest of it, well, we'll just have to do our damnedest to take them by surprise."

Eddie arrived back at the ranch just a few minutes after Slocum and Julia had left. When Bobby and Myrtle filled him in on what had happened, his face took on a long and worried look. "Y'all think we ought to go after them?" he asked.

"Slocum said no," Bobby answered.

"He said that might be just what they want us to do," said Myrtle. "If we all leave the ranch at one time, then they can take it back. He told us to wait here."

"Well," said Eddie, "it ain't going to be easy, but I reckon he knows best. His ideas have all been good so far."

"Let's go inside and have something to eat," Myrtle said. "It'll help pass the time." She continued talking as they all went into the house. "How'd you do, Eddie?" she asked.

"Everyone's coming," he said. "No one turned me down. Not a one."

"That's good," Myrtle said as she walked through the kitchen door.

Bobby and Eddie took their seats at the table. "It's good," said Bobby, "if we have Charlie and Slocum back here in time."

Julia slowed the pace and suddenly looked cautious. When she spoke to Slocum, her voice was low. "It was right up there," she said, pointing straight ahead on the road. Slocum looked around. There didn't seem to be anyplace nearby where four men could be hidden in ambush. They must have taken Joiner away somewhere.

"Let's go," he said. "Easy."

They rode ahead again until Julia stopped them. She looked around desperately, taking in exact landmarks. "Yeah," she said. "Right here."

Slocum dismounted to study the signs on the ground. He found the tracks of six horses, the four Mexicans and Joiner and Julia, he figured. They were lucky that no one else had come along this road since the encounter. The signs were clear. He saw where Joiner's horse had fallen, and he saw where Julia's horse had taken off at a hard run. It helped that he already knew the details from Julia, but all the signs corroborated her tale. Then he saw something he didn't want to tell Julia, not just yet. It looked to Slocum as if one of the four riders had dragged Joiner away on foot.

Five horses had ridden off the road down a trail that appeared to be seldom used. The tracks indicated the mounts of the four Mexicans, Joiner's riderless mount, being led, and Joiner being dragged behind one of the Mexican horses. Slocum straightened up. "They rode off that way," he said. "You know what's down there?"

"You see the tops of trees off there in the distance?" Julia asked.

"I see them," said Slocum.

"Well, the trail drops off there into a valley," Julia said. "Mr. Thurman's cattle roam in there some, and there's an old line shack. Nothing much else."

"Then that must be where they took him," said Slocum. "My guess is that they'll be looking for us. They sure weren't worried about being followed. Their tracks are too clear. They didn't even try to cover them."

"What'll we do?" Julia asked, the desperation plain in her voice.

"Well," Slocum said, "the way the land lays, we can get considerably closer before they have a chance of spotting us. Let's ride on that way a spell and see what it looks like when we get in closer."

Slocum climbed back into the saddle, and they moved off the road and onto the trail. They rode slowly, watching the way ahead of them carefully. Slocum didn't think that an ambush would be possible for a while, but he knew that they couldn't be too careful. He wasn't very happy with the fact that he had a woman riding along with him into whatever was waiting ahead, but then he'd needed her along to find the trail. Now he couldn't leave her alone out on the road. Maybe he'd find a place to leave her hidden before he approached the shack.

He caught himself on that last thought. He was assuming that the Mexicans and Joiner would be inside the shack. He told himself that it was not wise to assume anything. There were trees ahead where the land dropped down into the valley. There would be plenty of opportunity for ambush there. He decided that he was being foolish. He was playing right into their hands. "Julia," he said, "we've got to get off this trail and find a wider way around to the shack."

"It'll take too long," she protested.

"Listen to me," Slocum said, stopping his horse. She stopped there beside him, a firm look set on her face. "We ride straight ahead into them trees, we're riding straight into a trap. They took him down there to draw us in. They're waiting for us. I'll bet on it. I want to get Chuckie out of there as much as you do, but it won't help him none if we get ourselves killed before we ever see him."

She took a deep breath and heaved a heavy sigh. "You're right," she said. "I'm just so worried about him, John." She braced herself for a new move, and pointed to the right. "Let go that way," she said. "We can cross over those low hills and ride along on the back side of them. Then we'll be able to cross back over and come down on the shack from behind."

"That makes sense, girl," Slocum said. "Let's go."

They turned sharply and rode straight for the low hills at a gallop. They would reach the hills that way without wearing out the horses, then cross over and walk the horses again on the other side. There was no more talking. Julia rode along slightly behind Slocum and to his left. Both were anxious. Both were worried about Joiner, wondering whether he was dead or alive, and if alive, what shape he might be in. They rode on.

At last they reached the hills, low, rolling, and spotted with clumps of scrub oak. In a short while they had crossed over to the other side. They turned back to their left to ride along parallel with the rolling hills. They would continue along this route until they were well past the line shack. Julia would know when they were there. Slocum relaxed a little. He figured that the Mexicans would be watching for them to come from the trail, the straightest way. Even if they figured it possible that Joiner's rescuers would sneak in from a different direction, they couldn't very well watch all directions, not just four of them with Joiner to deal with. Even so, Slocum kept a watchful eye on the ridge above him and to his left.

It was late afternoon when Julia stopped them. She pointed toward the ridgeline with her left hand. "The line shack should be right over there," she said.

"Okay," Slocum said. "Let's ride on a little farther." They continued for about another mile, and then Slocum led the way cautiously up to the ridge. At the top, he dismounted in a clump of scrub oaks, and Julia followed his lead. The two of them looked down in the valley at the shack, almost a mile back behind them. A thin whiff of smoke curled up from the chimney.

"Someone's in there for sure," Slocum said.

"It's got to be them," said Julia. "What do we do now?"

"Get your rifle," said Slocum as he pulled loose his own Winchester, "and follow me."

In a crouch, Slocum led Julia from one clump of trees or bushes to another. At last they found themselves just above the shack. Slocum pointed to a small corral tacked onto the side of the shack. Five horses were in the corral. "That's Chuckie's horse there," he said. "We got the right bunch, all right."

"So what do we do?" Julia said impatiently.

"We take a little time to study the situation," Slocum said. "We think on it. The last thing we want to do is something hasty. I'd sure like to know how many of them're inside that shack right now."

"How can we find out?" Julia asked.

"Only one way I know of," Slocum said. "Stay here and keep quiet and out of sight. I'll be back."

He stood in a crouch and started moving again along the ridge, but this time he was moving alone and toward the end of the valley where the trail came in, where he and Julia would have come in had they continued the straightest way to the shack. Soon he dropped down the side of the hill just a bit so as not to make himself too obvious up along the ridge. When he found himself ahead of the shack, he moved more slowly and carefully, watching ahead and looking occasionally back at the shack.

When he figured he was close to the trail, he stopped in a brush clump and studied the terrain ahead. The trees and the brush had grown thicker. He was just about to the place where he had anticipated an ambush. He crept through the brush, sometimes barely moving, keeping as quiet as possible. Then he saw him. A lone Mexican. Sentry, he figured. Likely he was supposed to hurry back to the shack to report if he saw anyone coming. They would have plenty of time to get all four of them back up there in ambush position before any approaching riders had reached the crucial spot on the trail. He hoped he was right, and that there were no others hidden up there. He crept forward.

Here was a chance to cut the enemy force down from four to three, but he couldn't afford a gunshot or anything else that might alert the other three in the shack. He had to move as slowly as a snake creeping up on an unsuspecting mouse or a cat stalking a bird. Closer, he could see that the man under the big sombrero was sitting on the ground. He was smoking a cigarette. Slocum crept closer still.

The brush became thicker, and he laid his Winchester

down flat on the ground. It would be no use to him in this thicket; in fact, it would get in his way. He would pick it up later when he was finished with this chore. He inched his way forward. At last he was close, close enough to make a swift move and take the man out, but he wanted to do it in such a way as to keep the man from crying out or squeezing off a shot that would alert his *compadres*. Slocum's fingers found the haft of his bowie knife there at his waist It was not a weapon he favored, but there were times when nothing else would do.

Just then the sentry let fly a great fart and sighed audibly afterward. Slocum's face wrinkled as the vile odor wafted back to his nostrils. Suddenly angry, he pulled the knife, leapt forward, and plunged it into the man's back. "Ah," the man said, and then he relaxed with a final long sigh. He was dead. Slocum held his breath as he picked up the man's rifle and pulled his pistol out of its holster. Then he turned around and started on his way back to Julia.

Julia felt her heart beat faster when she saw Slocum coming. He was carrying two rifles. That could mean only one thing, she thought. She wanted to call out to him, but she knew better. Soon he was back by her side. "What happened?" she asked.

"I found their sentry," he said. "That means two things for us. One, we only have three to deal with now. Two, they're not going to be watching too carefully from the shack. They think they have the trail covered."

"All right," she said. "What now?"

"The sun's getting low enough," Slocum said, "and we're on the back side of the shack. I think I'll slip down there and spook their horses. That ought to bring them outside. You stay here, but if you get a clear shot at one of them, take it."

Without another word, he started down the hill headed straight for the shack. Julia made a move as if to say something to him before he left her, but she didn't know what she would say. She let him go. She checked her rifle, making sure a shell was in the chamber and it was ready to fire. She settled herself into a comfortable position from which to shoot. She raised the rifle to her shoulder, making sure she had a good shot at the shack. She was ready. She waited.

At the bottom of the hill, Slocum stopped. There was no cover from where he stood to the corral, but there was no window in the back wall of the shack. He should be able to make it all right. His hope was that the three men in the shack would hear the horses breaking loose and think that some critter had spooked them. He hoped that they would have faith in their sentry and not expect any rescuers out there. Then maybe all three would come out to catch the horses.

The corral was right up against the side of the shack to Slocum's right. He steeled himself and ran for it. He made for the back of the shack. Then he stood there for a moment, waiting to hear if he had made enough noise to cause an alarm inside. There was no indication that he had. Slowly he edged over to the corner of the shack, and slowly he peered around the corner. He saw the five horses milling around in the rough corral. There was no gate on the log corral, just a pole laid across the opening in the fence, but it was on the front side. It could be tricky.

He ducked under the back fence and started to make his way through the horses. One nickered nervously, and the nervousness spread. They all began fidgeting, stamping and moving around the small corral. He dodged his way through them to the pole at the front. Peeking around the front corner, he saw no one coming out the front door of the shack. Quickly he lifted the pole and tossed it aside. It made a loud ringing sound as it hit the ground. Slocum went fast back into the midst of the horses, whipped the hat off his head, and slapped at them. All five ran neighing out of the corral. He threw himself against the wall and pulled out his Colt.

"Qué pasa?" he heard from inside the shack. Then he heard the sound of the door being thrown open. Rapid footsteps followed. "Hey, *caballo,*" someone hollered. The horses had run in front of the shack, and though Slocum could not see what was happening there, he figured that the men were chasing them in that direction. Then one man came running around the shack on the corral side. He stopped, startled, and reached for his side arm. Slocum fired one shot that blew a hole in the man's chest. The secret was out, and Joiner's life was in the balance. Slocum ran for the front of the house.

The other two men had already run a ways out from the shack chasing horses. The sound of the shot had stopped them. They turned, pulling out their pistols. Slocum fired at one, and the man screamed in pain as a red blotch appeared on his thigh. Slocum cursed himself for having made a too-quick shot. He thumbed back the hammer to take a more careful aim. The wounded man fired a shot at him that kicked splinters from the wall into his cheek. "Damn," he snarled, and squeezed off another round. It tore into the wounded man's chest and dropped him instantly.

Slocum swung his Colt around for more action, but the last man had run out a distance, too far for an accurate shot from a handgun. The man was aiming a rifle at Slocum. Slocum knew it was a long shot, but he had no choice. He aimed the Colt carefully. There was a loud crack, and the Mexican staggered back a couple of steps. His rifle slipped from his hands and fell to the ground. Then his knees buckled, and he fell forward on his face. Slocum turned and looked up to the hilltop behind him. He smiled and waved his hat at Julia.

12

Julia grabbed up the three rifles: her own, Slocum's, and the extra one Slocum had secured, and hurried back to where she and Slocum had left their horses. Mounting up and leading Slocum's Appaloosa, she headed down the hill toward the shack. Slocum, in the meantime, had run around to the front of the shack. He found the door standing open wide. Sidling up to it, he peered around the corner. He heard Joiner's voice before he could see him.

"John," Joiner said, "I knew you'd get the bastards."

Slocum went on inside, where he found a battered and bloody Joiner tied fast to a straight chair. He moved quickly around behind Joiner, pulled out his still-bloody knife, and cut the ropes that bound him there. "Damn, boy," Slocum said, "those bastards really worked you over. Can you stand up?"

"Hell, yes," Joiner said. He stood and his knees buckled. Slocum grabbed him by the shoulders to keep him from falling. Then he lowered him back to the chair. "Take it easy, Chuckie," he said. "Don't hurry it. Is anything broke?"

"No," Joiner said. "I don't think so. I'm hungry as hell."

Just then Julia came rushing into the shack. "Charlie," she said. She ran to him and dropped down on her knees.

Looking up into his eyes, she said, "What'd they do to you?"

"I'll be all right," Joiner said. "It's just mostly scrapes and bruises, but I'm sure hungry."

"I've still got the food we packed," she said, standing up. "I'll get it."

"You stay put," Slocum said. "I'll fetch it in."

"It's in my saddlebags," she said. Slocum went outside.

"Oh, Charlie," Julia said, "I was so worried about you. I didn't know if they'd killed you or what. Damn. I wish they were alive again so I could kill them again."

"I'm just as glad they're dead," Joiner said. "Did John get all four of them?"

"He got three," she said. "I got one."

Joiner smiled down at her. "Good for you," he said.

Slocum came back in with Julia's saddlebags. He tossed them on the table, and Julia moved over to start rummaging through them. Soon Joiner was eating as fast as he could. Julia and Slocum let him eat as much as he wanted before they helped themselves to what was left. Finally Julia said, "You need some cleaning up, Charlie." While she got water and rags and started to work on Joiner's face, Slocum found the coffeepot and coffee the four Mexicans had left behind and made some coffee.

Joiner looked a little better after Julia had finished with him. His clothes were still dirty and ragged, but that couldn't be helped. Slocum put three cups of fresh, steaming coffee on the table and they gathered around to drink it. "How you feeling now, boy?" Slocum asked.

"I feel a lot better," Joiner said. "I reckon I'll be sore for a few days, but right now I feel pretty good. I can ride and I can shoot."

"The only riding you're going to do is to home," Julia said.

"And we ought to get started pretty soon," Slocum said. "I wonder how many more new gunhands old Harman has got."

"What?" Joiner said. "Oh. You think these four was Harman's men?"

"Who else?" Julia said.

"They wasn't Harman's men," Joiner said. "John, the last time we met up with these four, you made them take off their pants."

"Those *rurales*?" Slocum said. "Well, I'll be damned. Sons of bitches sure knew how to hold a grudge, didn't they?"

Joiner burst into laughter, and Slocum joined him. When at last their laughter subsided, Julia said, almost angrily, "What's so damn funny? Who were those men anyhow?"

"I'll tell you all about it later," Joiner said.

"They was just some old friends from south of the border," Slocum added, and he and Joiner laughed again. "Well," Slocum said, "maybe there ain't quite as much hurry as I thought. I think I'll go out and round up their horses—and yours. Gather up all their firearms and ammunition. Maybe we'll sleep here until early morning. Then head back."

"What about the bodies of those men?" Julia said.

"The crows and buzzards need to eat too," said Slocum.

"And coyotes," said Joiner.

Slocum sauntered on outside. By the time he had cornered all the horses and put them back in the corral, picked up all the loose guns and ammunition, and trudged back to the shack, it was full dark outside. He found Julia and Joiner sitting on the edge of a bunk, Julia cuddling Joiner's head against her ample bosoms. A lantern sat on the table burning low. There was still coffee on the stove, so Slocum poured himself a cup. He wished he had a bottle of whiskey. He did, however, have a cigar in his pocket. He pulled that out and lit it. Then he sat down at the table.

"How you feeling, Chuckie boy?" he asked.

"Aw, I'm all right," Joiner said.

"Well," Slocum said, "in just a bit I'm going to roll out my blankets outside. It's a mite too stuffy in here."

"I think I'll do the same," said Joiner. "I've been inside this damn shack too long now. Way too long."

"You sit still," Julia said to Joiner. "I'll go out and fix our blankets. Then I'll come back and get you."

Slocum smiled. He recalled the way Myrtle had pampered him when he was laid up, and he figured that Joiner must be enjoying this at least as much as he had enjoyed that. If a man had a good woman, he told himself, it paid to get a little hurt now and then. They sure could make over a man. Julia got up and went outside. Slocum finished his coffee and followed her out. In another few minutes, all three were bedded down under the stars.

It was still dark when Julia, the first to wake up the next morning, rocked Slocum by his shoulder. He moaned, rolled his head, and opened his eyes. "I think we'd better get started," she said. "I thought I'd let Charlie sleep until me and you get things packed up. Okay?"

Slocum agreed and crawled out from under his top blanket. "There's fresh coffee inside," Julia said. Slocum staggered into the shack and got himself a cup. While he sipped on it, Julia packed up everything of hers and Joiner's except the blanket on which Joiner was still sleeping. In a few more minutes, she got a cup of coffee for Joiner, carried it out to him, and knelt beside him. She put the cup down near his head, then leaned over and kissed him gently to wake him up. "Good morning," she said.

"Um," Joiner said, "good morning, darlin'." He raised himself up on an elbow, and then groaned out loud. "Oh, man," he said. "I knew I'd be sore this morning, but I didn't know how much."

"Can you ride?" Slocum asked.

"Oh, hell, yeah," Joiner said. "I ain't got no choice, have I?"

Julia said, "You do have a choice."

"What?" said Slocum.

"Well," she said, "as long as we've stayed around this

long, we might as well see if we can meet up with Mr. Thurman on the road. I'll bet he's driving a wagon or a buggy or something, 'cause I think Mrs. Thurman's planning to come along with him. Mr. Thurman also said he'd be bringing along some of his hands. I bet they're leaving about now. Maybe they've already started. If we ride out to the main road and wait a spell, they'll likely come along in a bit."

They polished off the coffee, packed up their things, and leading the four extra horses, headed down the trail. Julia rode close beside Joiner, sympathizing with his every groan as his horse jounced him along. It was still dark when they reached the end of the trail, but a sliver of light was showing along the eastern horizon.

"You think we're here ahead of Thurman?" Slocum asked.

"I imagine so," said Julia.

"I'd hate to sit here wasting time if you're wrong," Slocum said.

One of us could ride back toward Thurman's place and see if they're coming along," Joiner said.

"Same thing," Slocum said. "If they're already ahead of us that'd be wasting time. I wouldn't want you to be late for the meeting you called at your own place."

"So what do we do?" Julia asked.

"Well," Slocum said, "maybe we could wait a little while, but not for long."

"We won't have to wait for long," Julia said. "Look."

She pointed east along the road where the outline of a wagon and several horseback riders could be seen against the slowly widening strip of day light. "It must be them," Joiner said.

"Likely," said Slocum.

They waited patiently until they could at last recognize the riders. Julia said, "It's them, all right."

Thurman was surprised to see them, since they had been invited to spend the night at his ranch but had turned him down, so they had to give him a summary of the events with the unfortunate former *rurales*. Then, at Julia's pleading, they put Joiner in the wagon. Slocum was introduced to the Thurmans and to the six cowboys who were riding along with them, and then they all resumed the journey back to Joiner's ranch. Along the way, Joiner told Julia and the Thurmans the tale of what had happened in Mexico and why the four men had attacked him. When they had finished, Thurman said, "Now that we know all that, I have some news. Rather, Pete there has it. I'll let him tell you."

The cowboy called Pete rode out a little from the others. "Well," he said, "like I told Mr. Thurman, I was in town last night, and I dropped by the Hi De Ho for a couple of drinks, you know. I happened to overhear some of Harman's boys talking. Seems Harman give a wad of bills to one of his boys, the one they call Jelly, and Jelly's headed somewhere up north to try to round up some more gunhands."

"When did he leave?" Slocum asked.

"Well, that was last night," Pete said. "I reckon he's planning on leaving sometime this morning."

"Is there only one road north out of Rat's Nest?" Slocum asked.

"Just the one," Pete said.

"Tell me what this Jelly looks like," Slocum said.

"Aw, he's about my size," Pete said. "Wears a droopy mustache. He rides a little pinto pony."

"That ought to be enough to go on," said Slocum. "Now point me the quickest way from here to that road going north."

"You going after him, John?" Joiner asked.

"Seems like the smartest thing to do," Slocum said.

"What about the meeting?" said Joiner.

"You take care of it," said Slocum. "I'll get back as fast as I can. Now which way do I go?"

•   •   •

Slocum rode hard cross-country. He figured that he probably had plenty of time, but he wanted to make sure. If he could stop Jelly, they would still have only the nine remaining Harman men to deal with. No. Eight. Jelly would be out of the way. Eight, and that included Harman himself. If Jelly managed to get by, however, there was no telling how big a force Harman might gather with his money. Slocum was glad that Rat's Nest was such an out-of-the-way place.

From the directions he had been given, he figured that he had made it about halfway to the road north. He had to slow down his pace to save the Appaloosa. Part of him wanted to continue rushing ahead, but he knew better. He rode easy, the image of a rider on a pinto headed north occupying his mind. He tried to think of what he would do with Jelly if he caught him in time. Just kill him? Recalling the *rurales,* he thought about making Jelly strip naked and continue riding north, but then he also recalled the wrath of the *rurales* at their humiliation. No sense in setting someone else up for something like that. Better to kill him and not have to ever think about him again.

When he thought that he had walked the Appaloosa long enough, he urged him into an easy lope. Then a hard run for a while. Then back to a walk. Finally he reached the road. He moved out onto it easily and looked toward town. No rider was coming. He studied the ground carefully, and the tracks there did not seem to indicate that anyone had ridden past recently. The sun was moving up in the sky. Slocum moved off the road. There wasn't much cover, so he decided not to worry about it.

He pulled the saddle off the Appaloosa and let the horse loose with its reins trailing on the ground. Then he sat down beside the road and leaned back against the saddle to smoke the stub of cigar he had left. He made sure that his Colt was in a position where he could get to it easily. He smoked and he waited.

By the time the cigar stub was gone, the sun was halfway

up the eastern sky. Slocum figured it to be around ten o'clock. The meeting was just about starting at Joiner's ranch. He wondered if Jelly had left earlier in the morning than they had supposed, or maybe even the night before. Then he saw a rider coming. He saw that the man was on a pinto. It must be Jelly. He stayed sitting there beside the road, seeming relaxed. He waited for the rider to arrive.

When Jelly rode up even with Slocum, he stopped his horse, his right hand resting on the butt of his revolver. He looked hard and curiously at Slocum just sitting there. "What you doing there, stranger?" he asked.

"Resting," Slocum said. "Anything wrong with that?"

"I guess not," Jelly said. "You from around here?"

"Just passing through," Slocum said. "Say, you got a cigar on you?"

Jelly reached for his pocket, then stopped. "Say," he said, "why would I want to give you a cigar anyhow?"

Slocum shrugged. "They call you Jelly?" he asked.

"How come you to ask that?" Jelly said.

"If you're Jelly," said Slocum, "someone told me that you'd be riding this way. Said you was looking for good gunhands."

"Who told you that?" Jelly demanded.

"Just some feller I run into this morning," said Slocum. "Is it true?"

"Who wants to know?" said Jelly.

"Just an out-of-work gunfighter," Slocum said.

"You don't look like no gunfighter to me," said Jelly. "Sitting in the dirt and bumming cigars from anyone comes riding along."

"You want to try me?" Slocum asked. He put his hands out to his sides, so he wouldn't appear to be threatening. Then he stood up. "Pick me a target, and I'll show you."

Jelly looked up the road. "See that there big rock off to the right side of the road?" he asked.

"Yeah," said Slocum.

"Well, then, do you see the little one just in front of it?" Jelly said. "Let me see you hit that."

Slocum pulled his Colt and fired, and the rock bounced. "How's that, pard?" he asked. "You think I'll do? I could sure use a job."

"Ah, I don't know," Jelly said. "I don't know you. Mr. Harman might not like it me bringing back a stranger. What's your name anyhow?"

"What's a name matter?" said Slocum. "I could tell you Smith or Jones or any damn thing. Slocum maybe."

"It might matter to Mr. Harman," said Jelly. "I—Wait a minute. Say, I heard that Slocum name before. You Slocum? You work for Joiner?"

Slocum stood facing Jelly. He didn't answer the last question. He dropped the Colt back in its holster and watched Jelly's face. Jelly suddenly slapped at his revolver, but Slocum's Colt was out and blasting before Jelly could even clear leather. One slug tore into Jelly's ribs just under his armpit. The second drove its way diagonally through his chest to exit through his left shoulder blade.

"Ah," he cried. He jerked in the saddle. His head rocked loose on his shoulders. Then he slumped forward onto the neck of his pinto and hung there limp and dead. Slocum holstered his Colt and walked over to steady the pinto. He looked at the carcass hanging there. "I sure hope you was Jelly," he said. He led the pinto off the road, then dumped Jelly's body onto the ground. Kneeling beside the body, he gave it a quick search. He found a few cigars in the shirt pocket, and he took them out and stuck them in his own. There was a little money in the man's pockets, but not much. He pulled the revolver out of the holster and tucked it into his own waistband. Then he stood and walked back to the pinto.

Checking the saddlebags, he found the real money. He didn't bother counting it, but he could tell that it was a large sum. He stuck it back in the saddlebags, took the reins of the pinto, and walked to his Appaloosa. Then he mounted up and, leading the pinto, headed back toward Joiner's ranch. With a certain amount of pleasure, he thought that Joiner's ranch might be short of cattle, but all of a sudden it was developing a pretty good horse herd. Then he thought of the money in the pinto's saddlebags. Logic said that Harman had earned it at least partially from Joiner's ranch, so as far as Slocum was concerned, the money was Joiner's. The little shit can afford to pay me something now, he told himself.

13

When Joiner and Julia arrived back at the ranch, along with Brick Thurman and his crew, there were already some other ranchers who had come for the meeting. They were gathered there on the porch. "Sorry we're late, folks," Joiner said.

Hindman said, "My God, Charlie. What happened to you?"

Myrtle rushed down off the porch. "Where's John?" she said.

Thurman said, "Hold it now. We can't answer everything at once."

Joiner said, "John's all right, Myrtle. He'll be along directly. Let me get down out of this wagon and go get myself cleaned up a bit, and Julia and Brick maybe can tell you everything that happened."

Hindman helped Joiner down when he saw how stiff Joiner was, and then Joiner climbed the steps to the porch with moans and went on inside the house. A couple of men helped Julia out of her saddle and up onto the porch. "I'll get you some coffee," Myrtle said. Bobby gave Julia a chair, and everyone gathered anxiously around her. The Thurmans and their cowhands made it quite a crowd. Brick

Thurman walked over to stand behind Julia. He raised his hands to quiet the crowd.

"We were headed back here yesterday," Julia said, "from Mr. Thurman's place. We met four riders on the road, Mexicans. They attacked Charlie, and Charlie made me run for it. I came back here and got John Slocum. I guess most of you don't know John, but he's been helping us. So we rode right back out there, where me and Charlie had been jumped, and we found them in that old line shack of yours." She looked up at Thurman when she said that.

"My west line shack," Thurman said. "Most of you know where that is."

"I know it for sure," old McCulley said. "Wintered there for you once years ago."

"Go on, Julia," said Thurman.

"Well," she said, "there's not much to tell from there. We sneaked up on them, and killed them all and rescued Charlie. They had beat him up real bad, but he's all right, I guess. It's just scrapes and bruises. Anyhow, it was so late by then that we stayed the night and waited to meet up with Mr. Thurman this morning to ride on back."

"Mexicans, you say," Hindman said. "Was they hired by Harman?"

"That's what we thought at first," Julia said, "but it turned out they weren't. They were four *rurales* from south of the border that had an old grudge against Charlie and John."

"Seems Charlie and old Slocum had made them take off their pants and walk a ways," Thurman said. He and his cowhands, having heard the tale before, started laughing, and they were joined in what became raucous laughter by the whole crowd.

As the laughter was dying down, Myrtle came out to serve coffee all around. She started with Julia. "Thanks, Myrtle," Julia said.

"Sounds like I missed some fun," Myrtle said.

"I'll tell you all about it later," Julia said, "but you're just in time to hear about John."

Myrtle finished serving. "If you want any more," she said in a loud voice, "you can get it yourself. You'll find a pot on in the kitchen." Then she turned to Julia. "Now tell me about John," she said. "Why didn't he come back with you?"

"I can tell you that much," Thurman said. "When we met up with Charlie and Julia and Slocum on the road this morning, we loaded Charlie into our wagon, and Pete over there told them as how he had overheard in town that Harman was sending his man Jelly up north somewhere to round up some more gunhands. Slocum rode out to stop Jelly. We come on here. That's all we know."

"Then he wasn't hurt?" Myrtle said.

"Not when we last seen him," Thurman said.

"All right then," said Myrtle. "If he's just gone after one man, he'll be all right. He can handle himself."

Joiner came back out just then, wearing fresh jeans and a clean red shirt. Julia jumped up and ran to him to give him a hug. "You're looking somewhat better," Thurman said. "Get you a chair, son, and let's get down to business here."

Bobby drew up a chair next to Julia's for Joiner to sit in, and then stepped back out of the way. Someone handed Joiner a cup of coffee. "Thanks," he said. "And thank all of you for coming. I don't need to waste any time on the background of this situation. All of you know how Harman got this ranch away from me, and you all know by now that I've got the proof he was rustling all this time. You know why I've come back too. I wish John Slocum was here for all of you to meet, because if it hadn't been for John, we wouldn't likely even be sitting here talking. Most of what we've been successful at so far has been because of his ideas and what he's done. It was his idea to call this meeting, but I'll try to carry on the way I reckon he would have, 'cause some of you has come from a good ways off, and besides, we ain't got time to waste.

"Well, you know, Harman had himself a small army. Now, thanks to Slocum, we've got it cut down to nine, and that includes Harman himself. By the time Slocum gets back here, it'll most likely be down to eight. Seems like we ain't got too much of a problem left, but Slocum said we can't just go riding into Rat's Nest like a bunch of outlaws and attack Harman's Hi De Ho. It wouldn't look right, and some citizens might take it wrong and actual jump over to Harman's side before they figured out what it was all about.

"But the only law left for us is Eddie Cobb here, and if he was to go try to arrest any of them, they'd gun him down, sure as hell. That's what they done to Bud. So it seems that we have to go take them by force. We have to call them out and face them down. The reason for this meeting is that we want you all and everyone you know to be aware of what's going on. We ain't asking you to join us in the fight, just to stay to the side and help keep anyone else informed about it and out of it too.

"I figure we'll ride on in there, me and Slocum and Bobby and Eddie, and we'll call them out of the Hi De Ho and give them a chance to surrender to the law—to Eddie here. If they do, that'll be it. But I expect they'll fight first. We'll be ready for that. And we can take them too."

"Charlie," said Thurman, "what you said so far makes good sense, but when it's all over and done, how you going to get back your ranch legal-like? It's recorded now in Harman's name."

"I figure I'll do it just the way he done me," Joiner said.

Eddie Cobb stood up. "All Harman done is he paid the taxes when they come due," he said. "Charlie was hiding out in Mexico, and no one around here was bold enough to challenge Harman. We all just let him get away with it. It was that easy. Well, I don't believe anyone around here will challenge Charlie's right."

"They better not," McCulley shouted. "We'd skin them alive, by God."

"Anyhow, if anyone should challenge Charlie, in my capacity as the law, I'll just drag my feet about it till tax time comes up," Cobb said, "and then we'll let Charlie pay the taxes and he'll get it back in his name."

"That makes sense to me," Thurman said, and there were murmurs and some shouts of agreement from throughout the crowd.

"Only thing that don't make no sense to me at all," old McCulley said, "is why the hell you want to go in there after them just the four of you. Whyn't you let us all go in there? If that sleazy lizard Harman looks out on the street and sees all of us armed to the teeth a-challenging him, and him with only seven or eight men, he'll likely just come skulking out with his tail betwixt his legs. Then we can string them all up."

"I don't know about that," Joiner said. "I don't want no one getting hurt or killed over my problem. Besides, this was all Slocum's idea, and I don't want to say nothing more about it till he gets back."

Myrtle stood up and waved her arms for silence and attention. "Does that take care of all the business for right now?" she asked Joiner.

"I reckon so," he said.

"Then some of you men set up those long planks yonder to make a table out here in the yard," she said. "I've got enough food in the kitchen for an army."

"All right," Pete said, and he headed for the stack of planks.

"I ain't et no cooking 'cept my own for a hell of a long time," McCulley said. "By gum, I'm ready for some good eats."

"If you think you're ready," Hindman said, "what do you think about me? I'm sick nigh to death of your cooking."

Julia, Mrs. Thurman, and McCulley got up to follow Myrtle into the kitchen to help bring out the meal just as Slocum rode up leading the pinto. Bobby followed him to the corral and unsaddled the pinto while Slocum saw to his own Appaloosa. "Glad to see you back safe, Slocum," Bobby said. "Guess the other side's down to eight now."

Slocum said, "That's right. Hand me those saddlebags there, will you?" Bobby picked up the saddlebags from the pinto and held them out to Slocum. Then the two of them walked together toward the crowd, which was now seating itself along the makeshift table on the benches.

"Y'all," Bobby shouted as they approached the table, "this here's John Slocum."

Slocum nodded as he received howdies from all around the table. He walked over to Joiner where he was sitting and handed the saddlebags to him. "Hang on to this," he said. Then he looked at Bobby. "All these people and horses around suddenly made me nervous," he said. "We ain't never dug up all that dynamite we buried out there. You know, that stuff gets unstable after a while."

"You want me to dig it up now?" Bobby said.

"I don't think we need it anymore," Slocum said. "Get a couple of fellows to help you."

Bobby made his way over to the crowd of Thurman cowboys and said something to them. Pete and one other man got up and followed Bobby to the shed, where they got themselves some shovels. Soon the three of them were digging at each of the remaining short flags in the yard. McCulley and the three women started coming out of the house with trays and platters and bowls. Slocum took a place at the end of one of the benches. He watched as the cowhands pulled the bundles of dynamite sticks out of the holes and headed back toward the shed with them.

Bobby led the way into the shed. Pete went in next. As Bobby and Pete were headed back toward the table, the third cowboy went into the shed with his bundles. Alone in the shed, he looked over his shoulder. He was by himself. No one was watching. He pulled up his trouser leg and tucked a dynamite stick into his boot. Then the other leg. He tucked two more sticks inside his shirt, then walked out and back toward the table.

It took several trips back and forth between the table and the kitchen, but at last everyone was seated and eating. Myrtle had prepared a sumptuous feast, and as she had said, it was enough for an army. Everyone was well fed. The meal done at last, Brick Thurman stood up and called for attention.

"Mr. Slocum," he said, "we have a question to put to you."

Slocum said, "All right."

"Before you arrived," Thurman said, "we, this whole group here, volunteered to ride into Rat's Nest armed to back up your play when you call out Harman. Charlie said you didn't want us to do that. Will you tell us how come?"

"Mr. Thurman," Slocum said, "I believe that when me and Chuckie last discussed the possibility of such a thing, Harman still had a considerable number of gunmen backing him up. It didn't seem to me a good idea to cause a small war in town. Also, we didn't really know what to expect from all of you, so it seemed like the best plan to just tell you what our intentions was and how come. It seemed like it might be a more reasonable request than if we was to ask you to go get shot at.

"But the situation has changed, and if you all are actually volunteering to ride in with us, I for one would be just tickled to death."

A general cheer went up around the table. When it at last died down, Slocum said, "The real good part of this new approach is that it just might be the best way to avoid a fight. No one with half a brain would try to stand off this bunch with only eight men."

With the final step in the plan at last decided on, everyone seemed to relax. It was settled, and it looked like it was going to be easy. Myrtle finally got Julia to tell her tale of the events of the night before, and Slocum got Joiner off to one side to tell him about the cash in the saddlebags. Joiner, having had the law on his side for a change for a while now, thought that he'd better talk it over with Eddie

Cobb before claiming the cash as his own. Cobb said that he agreed with Slocum. The money was Joiner's. "Let's try to keep things as simple as we can," the deputy said.

The meeting was called back to order for one last piece of important business. "When do we do it?" Thurman asked.

"First thing in the morning," Slocum said. "I suggest that everyone stay the night right here, and we get an early start."

It was agreed. Mr. and Mrs. Thurman would stay in a guest room in the big house, and Bobby showed all the others to the bunkhouse.

The cowboy who had secreted four sticks of dynamite stopped Thurman just as he was about to go into the house. "Mr. Thurman," he said, "I'd sure like to ride on into Rat's Nest. I got me a little gal in there, you see, and I never knew that all this was going to come up. She's kind of expecting to see me tonight."

Thurman grinned. "All right, Andy," he said. "Go on in. You can join back up with us when we get into town in the morning."

"Thanks, Mr. Thurman," said Andy, and he headed for his horse.

They posted a guard that night on the front porch, but no one really thought they needed it. The eight outlaws in town weren't about to attack Joiner's ranch with such a force around it. Everyone was relaxed. They anticipated no problems with Harman and his remaining crew in the morning. Joiner and Julia went upstairs to their bedroom, and Myrtle followed Slocum into his room. As she shut the door behind herself, she said, "Hey, cowboy, you want some company tonight?"

Tonight and every night for the rest of my life, Slocum thought but all he said was, "Come on in, darlin'."

He was already out of his boots and shirt. He unfastened his jeans and dropped them to the floor, stepping out of them just as she came up to him to put her arms around him. They kissed passionately. Then Slocum broke loose from her and started pulling her clothes off to reveal her lovely nakedness. His rod was already standing up straight. Completely stripped, Myrtle pressed herself against him once more, and once more their lips met and parted. Their tongues darted in and out of one another's eager mouths.

Then Myrtle turned in his arms until her back was pressed against his chest, and his throbbing cock tormented the crack of her ass. He reached around her, taking a breast in each hand, and he pressed them, savoring the lovely smooth softness of them, soft yet firm. Then he slipped his hands down to her narrow waist, and she leaned forward, at the same time spreading her legs apart. Slocum slipped his cock down between her thighs, where he could feel her damp and hairy crotch. One of her hands snaked back and took hold of his tool, guiding its head into the wet hole there. He thrust forward, deep into her waiting cunt.

"Oh," she said. "Oh, John, fuck me hard."

He rammed his pulsing cock deep into her pussy again and again, slapping his pelvis hard against her round butt cheeks. "Oh, oh, oh," she said in time with the slap, slap, slap of their bare flesh as he humped her over and over again. The pressure built in his balls, and his cock felt ready to burst. He pounded harder and faster, and then he exploded deep inside her velvety cavern of delight. "Ahhh," he said, slowly relaxing.

He felt his legs weakening, and so, reluctantly, he backed out of her until his cock head slipped free. Then he turned and dropped down onto the bed. She crawled in on her hands and knees beside him and kissed him on the lips. "I'll clean you up," she said.

"The towel's over on the table," he said.

She nuzzled his chest and then his stomach. "I don't need it," she said, and then her tongue reached out and licked the length of his shaft. His whole body twitched at the sensation. She licked it again and again, then the area around it, cleaning the love juice off his body the way a mother cat cleans its young. She licked his balls and between his legs.

At last she took the entire length of his shaft into her mouth. She lolled it around, licking and sucking, and Slocum felt it begin to come back to life. She did too, and she bit down on it gently, scraping its length with her teeth. It stiffened, ready to go again, and she sucked deep until the head was in her throat, her face was pressed against his belly, her chin nudged his ball sack, and his crotch hairs tickled her nose. She backed off again, sucking as she did, until only the head was still in her mouth. Then she loosened the grip of her lips and plunged her head downward again.

This time Slocum thrust upward with his hips, ramming his cock into her mouth and down her throat. She pulled back again as his hips relaxed. Again she plunged, and again he thrust. He reached down with both hands, tangling his fingers in her hair, and now as he thrust and she plunged, he also shoved her head down and then pulled it back up. She sucked his cock. He fucked her face.

"Um, um, um," she moaned with each stroke. It was all the noise she could make with her mouth so full. "Um, um." Clutching her hair in two fistfuls, Slocum suddenly rolled her over until he was on top of her. Now he thrust down into her mouth and throat. Now he was genuinely fucking her face. He didn't know if she could take that kind of action for long, but then he didn't need much longer. A couple more thrusts was all. He felt it build, and he felt the sudden release. He shot his load deep into her throat. He pulled back and thrust again, but not se deeply as before. The second shot went into her mouth. She tasted it, savored the taste and the feel of it, and then she swallowed it.

When at last he pulled out, she reached up to take hold of the softening rod, which now hovered over her face. She squeezed and pulled and a final spurt shot out, landing on her cheek. She laughed, a gentle, musical laugh, and then she pulled the cock head back into her mouth for a final suck. She meant to get every last drop.

14

Andy Pride rode hard into Rat's Nest, and he pulled up just in front of the Hi De Ho. Quickly dismounting and slapping the reins of his tired horse around the hitching rail, he almost ran inside. It was late, and the place seemed to be deserted except for seven toughs. He knew them to be Harman's men. The word had already gotten around that the ranchers were gathering, he figured, and folks not involved on one side or the other were in their hidey-holes. He stopped still. The seven men all looked at him. Nervously, he walked over to the bar. He took a coin out of his pocket and laid it on the counter. "Whiskey," he said. The bartender put a glass and a bottle in front of him, and Andy poured a drink and tossed it down.

"I need to see Harman," he said.

One of the gunmen behind him said, "What about?"

Pride poured himself another drink. His hands were shaking. "I got information," he said without turning.

"About what?" the voice asked.

"About Joiner," said Pride. "About his plans."

"Tell me," the voice demanded.

"I'll tell Harman," Pride said. "No one else."

The voice said, "What do you think?" and another voice said, "That's Andy Pride. He works for Thurman."

"That right?" the first voice said. "That your name? Andy Pride? You work for Thurman?"

"That's right," Pride said. He swallowed the second drink and poured a third. "Will someone please tell Mr. Harman that I'd like to see him?"

Behind Pride the man who'd spoken second nodded toward the one who'd spoken first. That man walked casually to the office door and knocked. "Mr. Harman?" he said.

"What is it?" Harman's voice came through the door.

The man opened the door slightly, poking his nose in the crack. "A ranny out here wants to see you. His name's Pride, and he works for old Thurman. Says he's got some information on Joiner."

"Send him on in," Harman said.

Pride heard the words from over at the bar, and he turned to cross over to Harman's door. He felt smug, getting past the tough-talking gunmen like that. At the office door, the other man stepped aside. Pride stepped in and shut the door behind him. He took off his hat and turned to face Harman.

"Well," said Harman, "what is it?"

"Joiner had a big meeting out at his place today," Pride said.

"I heard about that," Harman said. "So what?"

"I was there," said Pride.

"So?"

"There was things discussed that you ought to know about."

"Are you going to tell me," said Harman, "or just stand there bragging?"

"I figure it ought to be worth something to me, Mr. Harman," Pride said. "I been a working cowboy all my life, and I ain't got nothing to show for it but just my horse and saddle and my six-gun and rifle and the clothes on my back. I got to think about my own self sometime."

"What do you want for your information, Mr. Pride?" Harman asked.

"Well, sir," Pride said, "I ain't no information peddler. I

ain't no sellout. But I figure that if I was working for you, well, then, I had ought to tell you anything I know that would keep you from getting wiped out. And if I was to keep you from getting wiped out, you'd keep on right here, and I'd have myself a good steady job—paying more than what cowboying pays."

"That's good thinking, Mr. Pride," Harman said. He pulled a wallet out of an inside pocket of his coat and counted out some bills. Pride's eyes opened wide at the sight. Harman held them out toward the cowboy. "This is a signing-on bonus, Mr. Pride," he said. "Is it satisfactory?"

"It's more money than I've ever held in my hand at one time, Mr. Harman," he said. "Yes, sir."

"Pull up a chair," Harman said.

Pride dragged a chair over to the desk and sat across from Harman. He leaned forward, anxious to talk.

"Now tell me what you know," Harman said.

"They're coming in here in the morning," said Pride. "First thing. Not just Joiner and his little group, but Thurman and half a dozen hands, old Hindman and his broken-down foreman McCulley—I'd say about thirty all told."

"Damn," Harman said. "That soon?"

"And Mr. Harman," said Pride, "if you're thinking about ole Jelly getting back here with more hands, well, you can forget that. Jelly ain't coming back. Slocum's killed him."

"Slocum?" Harman said. "Who the hell is Slocum?"

"A pard of Joiner's," said Pride. "Seems like to me he's the one that's really been running things out there. It was his idea to poke guns out all the windows and to plant the dynamite out in the yard."

Harman recalled the reports of a small army at Joiner's ranch with a cannon. Fools, he thought. They were taken in by a bluff. "Dynamite, huh?" he said.

"Yes, sir," said Pride.

"Well, I can't stand up against thirty," Harman said. "Not with just those seven out there and me and you. I'll have to pack up and get out right now."

"Unless you was do to them what they done to you," Pride said.

"What do you mean?" Harman said.

"Well, sir, you could poke guns out all the upstairs windows in town," said Pride, "and if that don't run them off right there, you could toss a stick of dynamite or two right down into the big middle of them. That can cut down the size of a gang real fast."

"I got no dynamite," Harman said. "What I had was all out at the ranch. It's in Joiner's hands now."

Pride grinned and reached under his shirt. He pulled out a stick of dynamite. "Not all of it," he said. He laid the stick on the desk and then pulled out another. He reached down to hike up his trouser leg, and he produced a third stick out of his boot. Then, from the other boot, he produced a fourth stick. He had them all lined up neatly on Harman's desk. Harman rubbed his chin and studied the sticks.

"You might have something there," he said. He stood up and walked around his desk toward the door. "Pick those things up and follow me," he said. Out at the bar, Harman called the other seven men around. "Boys," he said, "this is Andy Pride. We got some visitors coming in the morning, and they ain't friendly. As of right now, Andy here is in charge of the defenses. He's your boss. Do whatever he tells you to do to get ready for what's coming in the morning."

Pride felt his chest puff up and his face beam. Harman slapped him on the back. "Take over, Andy," he said, and he turned to walk back into his office. As he shut the door behind himself, he turned and locked it. He didn't want to be disturbed. He went back around to the business side of his desk and opened a drawer. He took out some money and stuffed it in his pocket. From another drawer he got a revolver, which he dropped in a side pocket of his coat.

He got up and moved to a safe off to his right. He knelt to work the combination and open the door. Then he dragged a satchel around, and began stuffing it with money. Anything else he might need, he could buy new, he figured. All he had to do was get out while the getting was good. That stupid Pride thought that he could simply duplicate the trick that this Slocum had pulled. Why, if it was Slocum's own trick, then Slocum would figure it out in a minute—or less.

So let Pride keep those seven out there occupied setting things up. Harman would use that time to slip quietly out of town. Then when Slocum's and Joiner's army got into town, Pride's stupid little defense would hold them for a while. Not for long, though. The dynamite was the best thing. Hell, Pride and the others might blow up half the town. Then Joiner's bunch would be kept busy looking through the mess to see if they had managed to get Harman. That would give him more time to get safely away.

He closed the satchel and buckled its strap, then moved over to the window that opened onto the alley behind the Hi De Ho. He shoved it up, stuck his head out, and looked in both directions. The alley was deserted. Harman climbed out and headed for the livery stable. He meant to leave Rat's Nest far behind him on the fastest horse available.

"All right, boys," Pride said. "First thing, I want you all to round up as many rifles and shotguns as you can get your hands on and bring them right in here. Hurry it up now. Get to moving."

"There's only seven of us, eight counting you," said one of the men. "What the hell do we want with so many guns?"

"You'll find out soon enough," Pride said. "For now, you just do as you're told. You heard what Mr. Harman said. I'm in charge of this here operation. Now get to hustling. All of you."

Each of the seven men made at least two trips back to the Hi De Ho to dump rifles and shotguns on the table. At last, Pride figured they must have brought fifty guns to him.

Fifty outnumbers Joiner and the others, he told himself. That ought to scare them off. "All right, fellas," he said, "come on along with me." He led the way outside, and then pointed to the second-story windows all along both sides of the street. "You see them there windows?" he asked.

"We see them," said one of the men. "We ain't blind."

"I want a rifle or a shotgun barrel pointing out each one of them windows," Pride said. "Whenever that bunch comes riding in here in the morning, I want them to think that they're facing at least fifty armed men."

"There ain't fifty windows up there," said one of the men. "Not even counting both sides."

Pride was flustered a bit, but he took hold of himself right away. "Well, I know that," he said. "I can count. That's just the first step is all. Now get on it. Get a gun in every window."

"Most of them places is closed and locked up right now," said the man.

"Then break into them," said Pride. "Who the hell owns this town anyhow?"

Grumbling, the seven men started carrying the rifles and shotguns around town again. Done at last, they reported back to Pride. "Now put them in the downstairs windows," Pride said, "and face some out the back windows in case those bastards think they're going to slip up on our blind side."

Two gunhands carrying an armload of rifles each walked around to the alley behind the Hi De Ho. One of them busted the glass out of the first window they came to, then shoved a rifle in there, butt first. "Axel, what the hell do you s'pose got into the boss, anyhow," the man said, "putting that silly shit in charge of us here?"

"I'm goddamned if I know, Harley," Axel said. "Hey. Looky here."

"What?" said Harley, hustling over to catch up with Axel.

"This here's the boss's window," Axel said. "It's wide open, and he ain't in there."

"Likely he went out to the bar to get a drink," said Harley. He poked a rifle into Harman's office window, barrel protruding. Then he started to walk on. Axel put his armload of guns on the ground and grabbed hold of Harley's arm. "Hold up just a minute," he said. "Look in there. The safe's standing open. Harman wouldn't leave his window open and the safe open like that. Would he?"

"I don't know," Harley said. "Once he told us to mind that stupid Andy Pride, I wouldn't be surprised at nothing he might do."

"Give me a hand," said Axel, and he started to climb through the window. Harley shoved on his ass, helping him through. Inside, Axel stood for a moment looking around. Then, tiptoeing across the room, he checked the door and found it locked from the inside. He went over to the open safe and looked in. Then he went back to the window and climbed out.

"Well?" Harley said.

"Harley," said Axel, "you want to know what I think?"

"Tell me," Harley said.

"I think the boss has run out on us," said Axel. "I think he stuck that silly ass in charge to get us running around like this and keep us busy. Then he went into his office and locked the door. It's locked from this side, Harley. Only way he could have come out is through this here window. The reason he left it standing open is 'cause it's too high to reach up from out here and pull it back down. The safe's open, and there ain't nothing in it. He got us distracted with silliness, took the money, and run out on us, Harley, and if we stay here, that little shit out there will get us all killed in the morning."

"Let's go," said Harley.

"Hold it," Axel said. "Where you going?"

"To tell the others," said Harley, "and to kill that little shit Pride."

"Well, now, let's just consider that for a minute here," Axel said. "We could do that, for a fact. Then what?"

"Well, we—"

"How about this instead," Axel said. "We don't tell no one. We let Pride keep the others busy with his stupid chores. You and me goes to get our horses, and we track down old Harman. He's the one done this to us. He's the one set it all up, meaning to get out with all the money and get us all killed in the process. He's the goddamned double-crosser that needs to be killed. Besides, if we kill Harman, we get all the money. These back here'll all be killed by Joiner and them in the morning. Well, pardner, what do you say?"

"I say let's go kill Harman," Harley said, and keeping one rifle each, the two gunhands left the extra rifles and shotguns on the ground there beneath the open window to Harman's office and headed for the stable. Not wanting Pride and the other five to find out what they were up to, they were careful to stay in the alley and stick to the shadows.

In the stable, they found old Gorman sleeping, and they shook him awake. "What? What?" he said, rubbing his eyes.

"Did you see Harman come in here tonight?" Axel said.

"I ain't seen no one tonight," Gorman said.

"We coulda had a gunfight here, and he wouldn't'ta woke up," Harley said.

Axel jerked Gorman up to his feet. "All right," Axel said. "We know that Harman came in here tonight, so you figure out what horse he rode out of here. Hurry it up."

Gorman staggered and stumbled down the line of stalls, still rubbing his eyes. Finally he stopped. "The big black's gone," he said.

"All right," said Axel. "Now what's the fastest two you got left?"

"Roan over there, I'd guess," Gorman said. "Then probably that sorrel there."

"Get them saddled up quick," Axel said. He pulled Harley over to the side and spoke low. "Harman's on a strong, fast horse, and he's got a start on us. It's hard to say just how fast he might be moving. He thinks he's running away from Joiner and them, and he don't think they'll be after him till morning after the fight that's coming. So my guess is that he'll go easy on the horse. We ought to be able to catch up with him."

"Yeah," Harley agreed. "We sure ought."

"All right," said Axel. "Let's go do it."

Gorman had just finished the saddling, so Axel pushed him aside, and the two gunmen mounted up. Axel led the way to the back of the stable so they could ride out of town unseen. They watched the tracks carefully, and found that Harman had gone north. They followed.

Back at the Hi De Ho, Pride had the others gathered up again. "Hey," he said, "there's two missing."

"Harley and Axel," said one of the men. "They must still be poking guns in windows out back. That's where they went. Out back."

"Well, all right," Pride said. "We'll fill them in later. So here's the plan, boys. We'll wait right here at the front door, all except you there. You'll be upstairs with these." He laid out two sticks of dynamite. "You ought to have a cigar going so you can light them quick if you need to.

"Whenever that big army rides in here, I'll just step out the door and tell them to look around at all the guns that's trained on them, and I'll suggest they surrender. That way, no one gets hurt. If they do, then that'll be the end of it. If they want to fight, though, that's when you light the dynamite and toss it out right in the big middle of them. That'll blow the fight out of them, you bet you. You got it?"

"Yeah," one of the men muttered, none too enthusiastically.

"Well, now," Pride said, "you men can go catch a little

sleep. We got a big morning ahead of us. Be back here, though, by first light, and be ready."

The gunhands all sauntered out of the Hi De Ho, grumbling as they went. Pride was puffed up with real pride in what he saw as a job well done. He decided that he should report to Mr. Harman, so he walked over to the office door. Harman hadn't even bothered to open the door since he had placed Pride in charge. He had shown complete confidence in Pride's ability to take care of things. He deserved to be told that his confidence had not been misplaced.

Pride tried the door and found it locked. He knocked gently. There was no answer. He rapped a little harder. Still no answer. "Mr. Harman?" he called out. Then a little louder. "Mr. Harman. You in there? It's Andy Pride, Mr. Harman."

15

Pride stood at the swinging bat-wing doors of the Hi De Ho Saloon watching the street. It was early morning. The sun was not yet even lighting the far eastern horizon. He was anxious. He was nervous. He had seen the crowd that would be riding into town soon. He told himself that the four dynamite sticks would be an equalizer, even though he was planning to face well over twenty men with only five, six counting himself. Joiner and his friends had done it, he told himself. Well, so it could be done to them. He noticed that his palms were sweating, and he rubbed them on his trouser legs. It didn't work. They were still wet.

He pulled the revolver out of the holster at his side to make sure that it was sliding easy. It was the fourth time he had done that. He pulled it all the way out and checked the shells in the six chambers. He spun the cylinder. He put the six-gun back in the holster. Pushing the bat-wing doors, he stepped out onto the board sidewalk and looked down the dark road, listening for the sound of any approaching horses. Everything was quiet. Real quiet. It was way too quiet for Andy Pride's comfort.

He went back inside and looked at the two sticks of dynamite he had placed on the tabletop nearest the door. They were still there, just where he had put them. Of course, no one had been inside the Hi De Ho since he had arrived. Of course the sticks would be there. He knew how nervous he was, and knowing it bothered him and made it worse. Where the hell are them other boys? he asked himself. And where is Mr. Harman? They ought to all be right here with me by now.

Out at Joiner's ranch everyone was up bright and early. They were all dressed and all well armed. Myrtle, Julia, Mrs. Thurman, and old McCulley had prepared a huge breakfast, and everyone had eaten well. Outside, the men had all saddled their horses. Bobby saddled one of the ranch's horses for Thurman, since Thurman had arrived in a wagon. Slocum saw that Myrtle too was armed and mounted. He rode over to her side. "You don't need to be going along on this," he said. "It's going to be a lark. Hell, we got a small army here."

"If it's going to be a lark," Myrtle said, "then there's no danger, and I want to go. I want to see this thing finished."

"Suit yourself," Slocum said, "but if they do try to start anything in there, you keep back out of the way. I don't want nothing happening to you, lady."

"Oh, you don't?" she said, her voice coy.

"I surely don't, Myrtle," he said. "I got too many things I want to say to you and a whole bunch more things I want to do with you."

"I'll stay out of the way," she said. "I want to hear those things you want to say."

Slocum leaned over to kiss Myrtle on the lips just as Eddie Cobb, in front of the whole crowd, called for attention. Slocum gestured to the rear of the crowd with his thumb, and Myrtle rode back that way. Slocum rode on up to the front beside Joiner. Everyone quieted down.

"All right, boys," Cobb said. "I just want to say one thing. I ain't in charge here, except that I'm the only law we got left. I don't want no one getting shot if we can help it. Don't start shooting. If they'll submit to arrest, then that's the way I want it to go. I want it all legal and proper, if they'll let us have it that way. That's all."

He rode over and took his place beside Slocum. Slocum looked at him, then at Joiner. Joiner turned to look back over his shoulder. He took off his hat and waved it in the air. "Let's go to town, boys," he yelled.

Harman was walking the big black horse. He had ridden it hard out of Rat's Nest for a distance, then slowed. He was in a hurry to get himself as far from Rat's Nest as he could. It had been a shame to walk away from the ranch and the Hi De Ho and the nice rustling operation, but after all, he told himself, he had plenty of money. He had stashed away a small fortune while everything was working well. It could support him in high style for the rest of his life, or it could set him up nicely somewhere else in just about any kind of business he might like to try.

His ultimate destination was vague in his mind, but he thought that he would get himself to Fort Worth and catch a train to—somewhere. Chicago? New York City? Maybe San Francisco. The weather would be nicer out west. Yeah, he thought. Somewhere in California. He would be far from south Texas. Safe from the clutches of Texas law. No one would know him. He could start all over and do so in style and comfort. The more he thought about it, the more San Francisco appealed to him.

Some distance behind Harman, Axel and Harley rode hard. Harley, lashing wildly at his mount, was a little ahead of Axel. "Slow down, Harley," Axel shouted. "Harley. Slow it down, goddammit." Finally, Harley heard the message and responded to it. He eased up on the horse and slowed it to a walk. Axel rode up beside him. "You kill your damn horse," he said, "you won't never catch up with Harman."

"Aw, hell," Harley said. "I know it. I'm just anxious to get the double-crossing son of a bitch in my sights."

"You ain't alone there," Axel said. "Harley?"

"Yeah?"

"When we catch up to him," Axel said, "let's don't kill him right off. Let's make him real sorry that he run out on us like he done. Let's make him real sorry before we kill him."

"He'll be wanting us to finish the job," Harley promised. "Axel, I'm hungry."

"Ain't nothing we can do about that now," Axel said. "We didn't pack nothing to eat. We'll just have to wait till we're done with Harman. Then we can head for . . ."

Harley waited for Axel to finish his statement. "Head for what, Axel?" he finally said.

"Hell," Axel said. "I'm thinking. Ain't nothing ahead of us for a good long while. We sure as hell can't just ride back into Rat's Nest. We might stop at a farm or a ranch or something and ask for something to eat. Hell, once we've done old Harman in, we could even pay a little for a meal."

"Yeah," Harley said. "We could do that."

"Then, well, then I reckon we could double back a ways and head on over toward Flanders," Axel said. "That ought to be safe enough. We can lay up there for a bit and figure out where we might want to go."

"Out of Texas," Harley said. "That's all I care about. Any old damn where long as it's out of Texas."

"Hey," Axel said, "looky there."

"What?" said Harley.

"Right there," Axel said. "Horseshit. Get down and poke a stick in it."

Harley dismounted, found a stick, and jabbed it into the pile. He looked up at Axel grinning. "We ain't far behind him," he said.

The five gunhands had at last gathered around Pride behind the bat-wing doors. He felt a little better with their company. "I've done put the other two dynamite sticks upstairs by the front window," he said. "One of you can go up there.

When that bunch rides in here, they'll most likely gang up right out there in the street. I'll step out the door here and tell them to turn around and go right back where they come from. Course they won't. That's when I'll set off a stick here, and I'll toss it right out in the big middle of them too. Then whichever one of you is upstairs toss one right after that. We'll probably kill off half of them just like that, and the rest will be fucked up. If we still need them, we'll have another stick apiece. Shouldn't be no problems."

He sounded calm and confident, but he was really trying to convince himself as much as he was the others. He stepped out onto the sidewalk again. The sun was at last lighting the morning sky. They'll be along any time, he told himself. Any time now. He went back inside and looked at the gunhand nearest to him. "Has anyone seen Mr. Harman this morning?" he asked.

Harman looked at the sun, barely peeking over the horizon, and he thought that the Joiner bunch was probably just headed into Rat's Nest. It would take them a little while, not long, but a little while to deal with things there. Then they would discover that he was gone, and they would have to determine which way he had ridden out of town. By the time they actually got around to pursuit, if they bothered at all, he would be well on his way with a good head start. They'd never catch him. He felt pretty good for a man who was running away. He had just come to a clear running stream, and he rode over to it, letting the black horse drink. He swung down out of the saddle and knelt at the water's edge to quench his own thirst.

He had a good drink, but he realized that he was hungry. He wondered how soon he would feel safe enough to stop for a meal. There would be ranch houses and farmhouses along the way. He figured he ought to pass a few of them by, get a little further away before he slowed himself down that much. He wished he had thought to pack in some trail food, but he had been in a hurry to get out of town.

He straightened himself up and stretched. It was going to be a warm day. He pulled off his long-tailed coat, folded it, and threw it across the back of the saddle. He gathered up the reins, took hold of the saddlehorn, and put his foot in the stirrup. Just then he saw two riders top the rise in the road behind him.

"Say," said one of the gunhands in the Hi De Ho, "where the hell's Axel and Harley?"

Pride looked surprised. He looked around and counted the other five men, pointing a finger at each one in turn. "Yeah," he said, "there's s'posed to be seven of you, ain't there? Where is them other two?"

"And where's Harman?" the gunman said. "There's something about this I don't like."

"Go see if you can find them," Pride said. "You two. Go on."

One gunman went to the stairs and started up at a run. The other went to Harman's office and knocked on the door. He waited a few seconds, then knocked again. "Mr. Harman," he said. "You in there?" He tried the door and found it locked. Then he knocked again, louder than before, and he yelled out, "Hey, Harman."

He hurried back to Pride. "There's something funny here," he said. "The door ain't locked. I can turn the knob, but I can't open it. That means that it's latched on the other side. But I can't get no answer from in there. He's got to be there. He had to be to latch the door."

"But he won't answer?" Pride said, and he recalled his own failure to get an answer from Harman's office the night before. "Come on," he said, and the two of them went back to the office door. "Break the son of a bitch down," he said.

The gunnie bashed his shoulder against the door, once, twice. He felt it give a little. Then he reared back, lifted his foot, and kicked it hard. The door flew open, its latch hanging from loose screws. Pride rushed into the office. No one was there. "The window's wide open," he said.

"That ain't all that's wide open," the gunhand said. Pride turned to look at the man, and saw that he was staring at the safe. Its door was standing open.

"I guess now we know why that asshole had you take over," the gunman said. "He's took all the money and run out on us. He left us here to hold off Joiner and them while he gets away. He left us to get killed for him."

"No," said Pride. "He wouldn't have done that. He's around here somewhere. He's got to be. Come on. We'll find him."

"Ah, shut up," said the gunman. He walked back out to join the others at the bat-wing doors, just as the gunman came back down from checking the rooms upstairs.

"Nobody up there but whores," the man said.

"Harman's cut out on us," the gunman who had checked the office said. "He's took the money and run off. Left us here to face Joiner and them alone. And get killed."

"What about Axel and Harley, Stick?" one asked.

"I don't know," the man called Stick said. "All I seen was the office, locked from the inside, the safe empty, and the back window standing wide open."

"Wait a minute," said another. "Didn't Axel and Harley go around back last night with them rifles and shotguns?"

"I believe you're right," Stick said.

"What if they seen that open window," the other man said, "and they looked in and seen that safe?"

"Chickenshits are as bad as Harman," Stick said. "They went after him for themselves. Didn't let us in on it."

"What are we going to do?" one of them said.

"I don't know about the rest of you," said Stick, "but I'm getting out of here before that bunch from Joiner's comes in."

Pride stepped out on the sidewalk. Over his shoulder he said, "It's too late for that, boys. Here they come."

Harman drew the rifle out of its scabbard, cranked a shell into the chamber, and steadied it across the saddle. He

sighted in on one of the riders and waited as they rode
closer. Then he recognized them. Axel and Harley. Somehow they had discovered his plan and come after him, after
the money. He had pulled a real dirty double cross on them,
and he knew that he couldn't talk his way out of it. They
would have no mercy on him. None at all. He squeezed the
trigger. Harley jerked and slumped in the saddle.

"What the hell?" said Axel.

"I been shot," said Harley. "I'm hit bad."

Axel jumped off his horse and ran for cover at the side
of the road. "Where the hell is he?" he said.

Harley tried to sit up straight in his saddle. He looked
down the road and off to one side, and he saw Harman
there beside the stream, the rifle still aimed at him. "Down
there," he said. "By the crick. Help me, Axel."

There was another loud crack, and a bullet smashed into
Harley's forehead, splattering blood and brains out the back
of his head. His body jerked and flopped back to come to
rest on the horse's ass. The horse neighed and reared, and
the lifeless body slid off to one side and landed in the road
with a sickening thud. Axel wished that he had grabbed his
own rifle before vaulting from the saddle. At least he was
hidden from Harman. But Harman knew he was up there,
and Harman had a rifle.

However, Harman couldn't see Axel where he crouched
beside the road, and Axel had spotted Harman once Harley
had told him where to look. He could see him, but the
distance was too great for a shot from his six-gun. It was
a standoff. He figured that Harman wouldn't run for it, not
with a man just up on the rise who was after him. But then,
Axel couldn't go for his rifle without exposing himself to
Harman's deadly fire.

"Psst!" he said. "Come here, horse."

The horse was unconcerned. Axel thought about throwing a rock at it, but he knew that would only run it off. He
looked down toward the stream below. If he only had a

rifle. He'd have a clear shot at Harman, standing there in the open like that. He tried to study out a route of cover that might lead him closer to Harman, but he couldn't find one that he had any real confidence in. Maybe, he thought, after a while Harman would get back on his horse and ride off. Then Axel could get on his and keep following. He'd have his rifle then. He decided to sit tight, be patient, and wait it out.

With Slocum, Joiner, and Cobb in the lead, the riders from Joiner's ranch moved down the main street of Rat's Nest. When they arrived at the Hi De Ho, the three leaders stopped their horses and turned them to face the bat-wing doors. The remaining riders spread themselves along the street on both sides of the leaders. Eddie Cobb dismounted. "Harman," he called out. "Harman. You in there?"

Pride stepped to the door. "Harman ain't here," he said. "He run off last night."

Thurman's eyes opened wide. "Andy?" he yelled. "Is that you?"

"Yes, sir," Pride said. "I reckon it is."

"What are you doing in there?" Thurman asked.

"I was just checking things out for you," Pride said. "There's only five men left in here. The rest has all run off. Maybe I can talk these here into giving themselves up."

"What the hell are you trying to pull?" Stick said inside the saloon.

"Well," Pride said, "it would be for the best. You can't fight all of them."

"We give ourselves up," said Stick, "and we'll hang for rustling. I'd sooner get myself shot. But you ain't getting out of this either."

"Now, wait a minute," Pride said. "I ain't done nothing for Harman. Never had the chance."

"You joined up with us last night," Stick said. "Bossed us around too. Now you're trying to act like it never happened. Well, go on then. Go on out there and join them then, you little shit-ass. I'll blow a hole in your back before you get halfway across the street."

"We, uh, we could all go out the back window of Harman's office," Pride said. He realized that he had most likely made the worst mistake of his life the night before, and he wondered if he would ever be able to spend all that money Harman had given him.

Looking out the window, Stick could see riders at each end of the long line fanning out even farther. They were moving around the building. "Forget that," he said. "They'll be watching the back. We're trapped in here."

"Well," said Pride, "let's give ourselves up."

"I ain't going to hang," Stick said.

"Let me talk to them," Pride begged. "Maybe you won't hang. I got some money. We'll get you a good lawyer."

"Talk then," Stick said.

Pride moved cautiously back to the bat-wing doors. "Hey, out there," he said.

"We hear you," said Joiner.

"If we was to give up," Pride said, "would we all get us a fair trial?"

"I'll get you a fair trial," said Cobb.

"If we don't hang you first," McCulley said.

16

"There's our answer," Stick said.

"Well, I," Pride stammered, "I say we use the dynamite."

He didn't want to fight. He had only just barely joined with this bunch. He didn't want to die with them so soon and for so little. There was money in his pocket. Money he would never be able to spend. He could give himself up. He wouldn't hang. He had not rustled cattle. He had not killed anyone. But if he went out the door to turn himself over to Eddie Cobb, Stick would shoot him in the back. He had said so.

"I'll take the upstairs," Pride said. "I can drop one right down in the middle of them from there."

"Go on," Stick said.

Pride ran all the way. Just as he was about to go into the room where he had placed two sticks of dynamite, four women came running out of another room and flocked around him. "What's happening out there?" one asked.

"Is there going to be a gunfight?" said another.

"Ladies," said Pride, "just stay back out of the way. You'll be all right."

"But all those men out there," said one. "What are they doing? What do they want?"

153

"All they want is just the five men downstairs," Pride said. "They ain't going to hurt you."

"What about you?" one asked.

"I ain't with that bunch down there," he said. "I'm fixing to give myself up out this window here."

"You going out by the balcony?" one of the girls asked.

"That's my meaning," said Pride.

"Take us out that way too," said one.

"Look," Pride said, "I ain't got time."

"Come on," she said, and the four women pushed their way past Pride into the room. They were at the front window before he was. "Hey. Hey, down there," the loudest of the women called out. "Let us come down."

Slocum studied the situation. There was a balcony across the front of the building. The women could get out on the balcony, go to the far end, the end to his left, climb over the rail, and shinny down the post there at the corner. He told Joiner, "We best let the women out. We don't want them getting hurt."

"Sure," Joiner said.

"Have a couple of Thurman's boys go over there and help them down," Slocum said.

In another minute the first of the girls was climbing over the balcony. Slocum kept his eye on the bat-wing doors. The girls would be out of the line of fire unless one of the men inside were to step out onto the boardwalk. Slocum meant to see that didn't happen. Squealing, the first girl came down the pole into the arms of two cowboys. The second one, her skirt hiked up, was climbing over the rail. Andy Pride crawled out the window and walked to the edge of the balcony, his hands held high.

"Can I come down that way too?" he asked. "I want to give myself up. If I come out that door downstairs, they'll shoot me in the back."

"Come on ahead," Cobb said, "but after the girls are all down."

The third woman shinnied down to sit astraddle of a cowboy's shoulders. "Damn, Dottie," the cowboy said. "I never figured to have my head between your legs this morning." The fourth woman was swinging a leg over the rail, and the other cowboy was standing just below, getting his eyes full and getting ready to receive her down there.

Behind the bat-wings, one of the gunhands said to Stick, "What the hell's going on out there?"

"The whores is climbing over the balcony," Stick said. "And that little shit Pride is fixing to. He's give himself up."

"They'll be coming for us then," said the other man.

"Strike a match," Stick said, and he turned and picked up one of the sticks of dynamite. The man struck the match and held it out. Stick touched the fuse to the flame. It fizzled. It was lit. A sudden frightful thrill ran through the body of Stick as he stared at the spark-spurting twine. Then he stepped out through the bat-wings, raised his arm over his shoulder, and gave a mighty fling. The dynamite stick flew through the air. McCulley saw it and raised his rifle.

"Double-crossing bastards," he snarled, and sighting quickly on Pride up on the balcony, fired. The dynamite stick landed on the ground just behind Slocum. As Stick ducked back inside the saloon, Slocum threw himself off his horse. He hit the ground with a thud, rolled, and grabbed up the dynamite stick.

The women ran screaming for the perceived safety of the ranks of men across the road as Pride, staggering on the balcony, knowing that he had been hit bad, pulled out his revolver. He wanted to shoot someone, anyone before he died. He pointed toward the crowd of ranchers and cowboys across the street. He wavered. He fired.

Slocum tossed the dynamite stick right back where it had come from. It sailed neatly back into the saloon over the bat-wing doors. Up on the balcony, Pride jerked and twitched as a barrage of bullets smacked into his body.

Behind a row of Thurman's mounted cowboys, Myrtle slumped in her saddle, a red stain spreading over her left breast. She had caught the wild shot from Pride's six-gun.

Then there was a deafening roar as the front of the Hi De Ho exploded, sending dust and debris out into the street, showering the riders out there. Horses stamped and shrieked. The four whores screamed. Riders fell or were blown out of their saddles, and frightened, confused horses ran this way and that in the street.

Harman was growing impatient. He knew that Axel was up there on the rise, and he figured that he had left his rifle back on his horse. Otherwise, he would have been shooting. Harman thought about riding up there, but that would put him within Axel's six-gun range, and he didn't know exactly where Axel was hidden. He was safer right where he was. Maybe Axel would lose his patience and make a move for the rifle. Show himself. Then Harman could pick him off.

But wait, he thought. He can't hit me from that range with a six-gun. What if I was to just jump in the saddle and take off? It seemed like a good thought for only an instant. If he were to mount up and start riding, Axel would be able to run for his rifle and get a shot at his fleeing back. Even if he could ride off faster than Axel could take aim and fire, Axel would still be behind him and in pursuit. That wouldn't work. But suddenly he knew what would. He took careful aim across his saddle. His rifle shot echoed through the morning air. Axel's horse gave an almost human-sounding scream, reared, and fell hard to the ground.

"Goddamn," Axel said. A second shot rang out, and Harley's horse staggered and fell. "Son of a bitch!" Axel shouted. He stood in time to see Harman mount up and start to ride. Axel ran to the side of his fallen horse. It was lying on its side, partially pinning the rifle under its dead weight. Axel took hold of the stock with both hands and started to pull. He looked back in the direction of Harman, but Harman was racing away. The rifle came loose, and Axel fell over backwards. Scrambling, he got to his knees and picked up the rifle. Sighting desperately, he squeezed off a round, and he saw Harman's big black stallion jerk and kick. Harman fell off to the side.

"Now we're even," Axel said. Rifle in hand, he started walking down the road.

When the cloud of smoke and dust began to clear, Slocum, Joiner, and the others could see that the whole front of the Hi De Ho Saloon had been blown away. They knew that Pride had been killed up on the balcony. There wasn't much doubt that the others inside, gathered there around the front door, had been blown to bits by the blast. Slocum wondered if it would even be possible to figure out who all had been there and been killed.

"Goddamn," Joiner said.

"I reckon there ain't no one left to arrest," said Cobb.

"Likely you're right about that," said Slocum. "It's going to be damn hard to prove one way or the other, though." He recalled that Pride had said that Harman had run off the night before, and he reminded Cobb and Joiner of that fact. "Why don't we ask them girls?" he said. "They're the only ones left that was in the building."

"I'll do that," said Cobb. He dismounted and started walking toward where the girls had huddled up behind the Thurman cowhands.

As he approached, one of the hands in back called out to him. "Hey, Cobb. Lady's hurt back here." Cobb hurried on over to the cowboy who had called his name. Another cowhand was lowering Myrtle from the back of her horse. Cobb got to them just as they were laying her out on the board sidewalk. He could see immediately that she was hit bad. "Someone get Slocum over here," he said. He knelt beside her.

"Myrtle," he said. "Can you hear me?"

"Yeah," she muttered. Her eyelids were half down, and her voice was weak.

"Someone get a doctor," Cobb yelled. Then he lowered his voice again. "Hang on, Myrtle," he said. "We're getting help."

Then Slocum pushed through the crowd of cowboys and dropped down beside Myrtle. He lifted her head gently and cradled it. "Oh, Myrtle," he said. "Myrtle, it'll be all right."

"John," she said, her voice barely audible, "what were all those things you wanted to say to me?"

"I wanted to say that I want to spend a lot of years with you," he said. "I wanted to say I never before knew a woman I wanted to grow old with. I wanted—"

He felt her relax suddenly in his arms, and he knew that she was gone. Silently he cursed himself for not having insisted that she stay behind at the ranch. Now she was gone. Just like that. All that life and all that loveliness. Gone was the vision in his head with which he had been struggling. The vision of a home and a settled life. All gone. All because of one stray shot, the only shot that had been fired in their direction.

"Step aside," someone said. "Here comes the doc."

Slocum didn't bother looking up. "Never mind," he said. He still cradled her in his arms, and slowly and gently, he rocked.

Some of the men had gone inside the shambles of the Hi De Ho to see what they could see. "Here's a boot," one of them said.

"Here's one that ain't blowed apart," another one said. The body was close to the back wall, lying facedown and burned black all up and down its back. "He must have been running for it. Got farther than the others."

A cowboy wandered through the open door to Harman's office. He stood studying it for a moment. Then he stepped back out. "Say," he hollered. "One of you call Eddie Cobb in here, will you?"

Outside, Cobb had stepped aside to leave Slocum with his grief. He was a little relieved to hear his name called, and he strode on over to the wreck of the Hi De Ho. Walking in through the mess, he saw the cowboy in the back waving him over. He picked his way across the debris to the open office door.

"Look in there," the cowboy said.

Cobb looked. He saw the open window and the open safe. He walked over to look in the safe and saw that it was empty. "I guess ole Pride didn't lie to us," he said. "It sure looks like Harman flew the coop, all right."

He turned and went back outside, where he found Joiner talking with Thurman and some of the other ranchers. He walked over to them. "I guess it's all done here," he said, "except that it looks like Pride told us true. Harman's gone. His safe's standing open and so's his back window. Looks like he run out on his own boys. Course there ain't no telling how long it'll take us going through this rubble here to prove who was in there and died. Maybe we won't ever know. Far as I can tell, there's just one whole body in there. The rest was blowed to bits, I guess. Still, it looks like Harman got away. We ought to investigate that."

"He'd have had to get him a horse," Joiner said. "We can check down at the livery stable."

"Let's you and me go do that," Cobb said. "Should we say anything to Slocum?"

"Not now," said Joiner. "He's sitting over there with Myrtle—taking it pretty hard. Let's leave him be for a while."

Cobb and Joiner walked down the street to the livery stable, where they found old Gorman standing out front and staring down the street toward where the big explosion had taken place. "What the shit happened down there?" Gorman said as the two men approached him.

"Those old boys in the Hi De Ho tossed a dynamite stick at us," Joiner said. "We tossed it back."

"God A'mighty damn," said Gorman. "Who was they? Harman's bunch?"

"That's right," Joiner said.

"You see anything of Harman last night?" Cobb asked the old man.

"He come in here from the back way and took off with that big black stallion," Gorman said. "Left out the back way too."

Joiner looked at Cobb. "Just what we figured," he said. "About what time was that?"

"Ain't got no idea," Gorman said. "I'd been sleeping. He woke me up. I never checked the time."

"All right," Cobb said. "Do you know which way he rode out of town?"

"Never looked," Gorman said. "I went back to sleep."

"Well," Joiner said, "maybe we can find some tracks. Anything distinctive about that black horse's prints?"

Gorman shook his head. "Naw," he said, "but I reckon you could look for the prints of that little roan. She's got a nick in her left front shoe." He looked around a bit, then said, "Right here. See?" He was pointing to a hoofprint in the dirt.

Cobb and Joiner looked at the print. Then Cobb looked back at Joiner. "What do we want to be looking for this print for?" he said.

"Well, after Harman left," Gorman said, "two of his rannies came along and woke me up again. Axel and Harley's their names. They made me saddle up two horses for them. A sorrel and a roan, they was. They asked me if I'd seen Harman, and I made out like I hadn't seen nothing. But I reckon they was taking out after him for some reason. I surely do."

"Mr. Gorman," said Cobb, "thanks for the information. You've been a big help."

Cobb and Joiner turned to walk back toward where the others still milled around the scene of all the action, and Gorman hollered at their backs. "Does this mean that Harman and that bunch is cleaned out of here?" he asked them.

"Yes, sir," said Cobb.

"That's exactly what it means, Mr. Gorman," said Joiner.

"Well, hot damn," Gorman said, and he did a little dance. "Hot diggity damn."

Walking along, Cobb said to Joiner, "I got to go after them two. They're wanted for rustling, at least."

"Well, you ain't going alone, Eddie," Joiner said.

"Thanks," Cobb said.

Slocum had torn himself away from Myrtle's body and then not looked back. He would let someone else take care of it. He didn't want to see it. He tried to see her as she had been alive, but the image of her limp body in his arms would not leave his head. He was afraid that it never would. He felt a terrible rage rising up inside him over what had happened to her. He wanted to kill someone. He knew it would do no good, knew that nothing could bring her back, but that didn't matter. He wanted to kill someone. He remembered that Pride had said that Harman was gone. He hoped that was true. He could at least have the satisfaction of tracking that son of a bitch down and killing him. He was afraid that everyone else had already been blown to the winds.

He was standing on the sidewalk across the street from the wrecked Hi De Ho, and was just about to walk over to inspect it when he saw Joiner and Cobb returning. He met them in the middle of the street.

"Ain't no need for you to go in there, John," Joiner said. "Me and Eddie's already checked it out."

"What did you learn?" Slocum asked. His face was grim, and both of the other men could see it.

"John," Joiner said, "why don't you just take it easy for a spell? Go on back out to the ranch and rest up. We can handle the rest of this."

"What did you learn?" Slocum said again.

Joiner sighed, and Eddie Cobb said, "Harman was not in

there. He cleaned out his safe and ran out on his own boys, what was left of them. He got a horse down at the stable last night. We don't know what time. But after he left, two of his boys, Axel and Harley, went in the stable and got horses. They took out after him. We figure they had found out he run out on them."

"Which way did they go?" Slocum asked.

"We don't know yet," Cobb said, "but one of their horses has got a nicked left front shoe. All we need to do is look for its tracks."

"Let's go then," Slocum said.

"John," said Joiner, "you ain't fit to ride out after them just now. Not just after—"

"I'll go alone, or you can ride along with me," Slocum said. "Either way. I don't give a shit."

He walked back to where his big Appaloosa stood patiently waiting, and he mounted up. Turning the horse, he rode toward the stable.

"Come on," Cobb said, and he and Joiner ran for their horses.

17

Axel cranked a shell into the chamber of his rifle as he walked. Pretty soon, he figured, he'd be close enough for a shot, and he wanted to be ready. He saw Harman stagger to his feet, obviously stunned by his fall. As Harman stood swaying, Axel started to trot. He needed to get his shot off before Harman recovered sufficiently to pick up his own rifle. He picked up his pace. He wasn't quite close enough for a sure shot. He could see Harman straighten himself up, almost stretch, and shake his head as if trying to clear it. Axel watched as Harman, apparently recovered, looked up in his direction. Then Harman quickly retrieved his own rifle. Axel could see him work the lever, then raise the rifle up to his shoulder. Axel quickly jumped to the right side of the road and crouched behind a tree. A shot rang out, and Harman's bullet kicked bark from the tree trunk.

"Son of a bitch," Axel snarled, and he snapped a shot off at Harman. He could see it kick up dust a few feet to Harman's left. "Damn," he said. He knew he'd fired too quickly. Harman moved to his own right over behind a rock there at the side of the road. Axel looked around at the surrounding landscape. He had to find a way to get closer to Harman. The growth along the side of the road was mostly low and scrubby. There was another tree not quite halfway down to where Harman lurked, waiting for him. He decided to try to make it to that tree by crawling along in the low brush.

Dropping down to his hands and knees, he began moving slowly toward his new destination. Harman snapped off another shot, and Axel stopped still. He had no idea where the shot hit, but Harman must have seen him move, or he wouldn't have wasted a bullet. Axel dropped down flat and began to belly his way along. He cursed Harman silently as he crawled. He was tearing his clothes, filling his shirt-front with dirt and rocks and scratching himself up. He was already a fair distance out away from civilization without a horse. Now, even killing Harman wouldn't change that.

He wanted to kill Harman, though. He wanted to kill the man for having run out on him the way he did, for having stolen from him, for having put him in this troublesome and uncertain situation. He also wanted all that cash that he knew Harman was packing. He thought again about the possibility of finding someone's home not too far down the road. With Harman's money, he would be able to buy a horse, pay for a home-cooked meal, and never even miss the money he spent. He decided that he'd have to push those thoughts back out of his mind, as much as they were bothering him. He needed to concentrate on Harman, on getting himself close enough for a good sure shot and on getting a dead bead on Harman before Harman even saw him pop up to shoot.

Slocum, Joiner, and Cobb rode back to the stable, where they managed to locate the one telltale hoofprint. They followed it out of town, and soon they were able to determine pretty clearly that there were indeed two horses following a third horse. Axel and Harley following Harman. There seemed to be no question about it. "It's them, all right," Cobb said.

"Let's go get the bastards," said Joiner.

"They've got a pretty good head start on us," Cobb said.

"Yeah," said Joiner, "but when Axel and Harley catch up with Harman, they'll slow down for sure. They'll be having it out. Hell, if we're lucky, some of them will be killed already by the time we get there."

Slocum rode in silence. He hoped that the three weren't all killed. It could happen in a gunfight. He'd seen it before. This time, though, he hoped it wouldn't happen that way. He wanted to kill someone himself for what had happened to Myrtle. He didn't want to just see them dead. He wanted to do it personally. For a brief instant he thought that he should force himself to stop thinking about Myrtle and concentrate on tracking the three fugitives ahead and what he would do when he found them. Then he changed his mind. The more he thought of her, the more he remembered, the more he kept that final terrible image of her dying in his arms sharp and clear in his mind, the more determined he would be to catch them, and the more cold-blooded and hard and cruel he would be when he had them in his sights.

"We don't catch up with them pretty soon," Cobb said, "we'll be outside my jurisdiction."

"When that happens," Slocum said, "you just turn on around and go back to town. Both of you. I'll kill them myself."

It was the first thing he had said since they had started following the tracks out of Rat's Nest, and the harshness of it stung both of the other riders. They had been partners in this fight. They thought they were friends. Joiner, especially, wanted to snap back, but he kept himself quiet. He knew that Slocum was hurting. He knew why. They rode on in an uneasy silence after that. They rode easy. As bad as Slocum wanted to kill, he was in no hurry. He savored the hard-edged hatred that burned in his breast. It didn't need to be over with too quickly, this killing. The men they were tracking could run from him as far as they wanted to run. He would be right behind them, walking steadily. He would keep coming. No matter how far they ran, he would keep coming. Sometime he would catch up. Of the three fugitives, there might be only two left, or just one. Either way, Slocum would finish it.

Axel thought that he was at last close enough for a good shot at Harman. Besides, he was more than tired of crawling around on his belly. He raised himself up, rifle ready, but he did not see Harman. Harman had moved. He looked up and down the road, but he stayed up and exposed for too long. A shot rang out, and Axel felt something hot tear through his left ear. He yelped and dropped back down out of sight. Holding his rifle tight, he rolled hard to his right, away from the road. He rolled into deeper and thicker brush, and then he sat up quickly, alert. Where was the bastard?

He felt the hot sticky liquid running down his neck and under the collar of his shirt. He reached up to touch his ear and found it jagged, a piece hanging loose. The touch of it almost made him sick to his stomach. He jerked his hand away. It was sticky and wet and red-stained.

"You greasy asshole son of a bitch," he shouted. "You tore off my fucking ear. I'm going to gutshoot you. I'm going to shoot holes in both your kneecaps. Goddammit, I'm bleeding like a stuck pig from out of a hangy-down ear. I'll get you, you hog's ass. I'll cut off both your ears and wear them on a watch chain."

"You'll have to find me first, Axel," said Harman, and Axel, for the life of him, couldn't figure out just where the voice came from. He sure didn't want to stick his head up again for a look. He decided that he would have to change his whole approach to this problem. He began scooting farther away from the road and backtracking at the same time. He was moving away from Harman. Harman would expect him to try to get closer. It would take Harman a while to figure this one out, and by the time he did, maybe Axel would be already behind him in position to shoot.

Axel moved slowly, inching his way along. His wretched ear still bothered him, was still bleeding profusely. Axel wondered just where in the hell all the blood was coming from, just out of a little old ear. He never would have thought an ear could bleed all that much. He thought, with sudden horror, that maybe it was leaking out of his brain. He kept himself going anyhow. He was determined to kill Harman, or at least hurt the son of a bitch real bad, before he bled to death out of his ear.

He at last reached the place where his and Harley's horses had gone down. He crept back over to the road and peered out cautiously. Still, he did not see Harman. He hoped that Harman would not see him, would instead be watching for him to sneak closer. On hands and knees Axel scurried into the road, pulled loose the rifle from the scabbard on his dead horse, then scooted on across. He was now on the same side of the road as Harman was, or at least, the same side of the road where Harman had been. The son of a bitch could have moved. Axel looked back briefly at the carcass of Harley, flies buzzing around it already, and he thought that Harley, dead like that, looked pretty stupid. He started moving again, getting himself well off the road. The cover was pretty good there. He straightened himself up and started walking. He meant to come up right behind Harman and shoot him in the back.

Walking down toward Harman, Axel realized suddenly that he was winded, and his mouth and throat were dry and scratchy. He wished that he had taken time to grab a canteen of water from off one of the dead horses. Then he remembered that he and Harley hadn't even bothered to load canteens. They had thought that they would catch Harman easily, kill him, take the money, and ride on. He thought about the stream where Harman had watered. It was just down there, past Harman and on the other side of the road. He puffed as he walked, each puff of breath drying his mouth and throat even more. "Shit," he said. He felt as if he'd been eating dirt.

• • •

Cobb stopped his horse. "This is as far as I can go," he said, "legally. Course, I could keep on going with you, unofficially."

Slocum considered his own earlier abrupt comment on the matter of jurisdiction. He knew that his caustic manner had hurt both Cobb and Joiner. He didn't really want to do that again. He hadn't meant to do it the first time. He'd figured just at that moment that once he finished this chore, he would likely never see either one of these men again. He would just keep riding on—somewhere. There was nothing at Rat's Nest or Joiner's ranch for him. Nothing but painful memories. But these men had fought and killed with him. Well, he could part with them better than with an insult.

"Eddie," he said, "since you're the only law among us, I really need for you to go on back to your office and do whatever it is you lawmen do to make Harman and them other two into fugitive outlaws. Whoever I find alive out there, I mean to kill him. And like you said, I'll be out of your jurisdiction. That means I'll be in someone else's jurisdiction, and I might have to answer for that. You get my drift?"

"Yeah," Cobb said. "I think so. Well, I guess I can fill out some papers on Harman and them other two. Then send the word out on the wires about them. You know, wanted men. That sort of thing. Hell, I think I can even authorize a reward. I ain't sure about the procedure on that, but I think I can."

"You go on and do all that for me then," Slocum said. "And won't you be needing Chuckie boy here to sign something, like a complaint or something?"

"Well, yeah, I guess so," Cobb said.

"Aw, now, wait a minute, John," Joiner said. "I mean to see this thing through with you. After all, it was my fight that got you into this."

"It was a bushwhacker's bullet that got me into this," Slocum said, "but it's something else that's driving me on now, and it ain't got a damn thing to do with you or your ranch. It ain't even got to do with the bushwhacker no more. Even so, I don't want to get throwed in jail or hanged for it, so I need for you to go back with Eddie and take care of that legalistic paperwork. All right?"

"All right. John," said Joiner. "When you're done, come on back to the ranch. Okay? You got yourself a home there for as long as you want it. You know that. You will come back, won't you?"

Slocum looked from Joiner to Eddie Cobb. "Eddie," he said, "if you do come up with a reward, use it for her funeral." He then turned back to Joiner. "I'll be seeing you," he said. They shook hands warmly all around, and then Slocum nudged his big Appaloosa forward. He did not look back again. Joiner and Cobb sat still watching him for a long, silent moment.

"Eddie," Joiner said, "he ain't coming back. You know that, don't you? We'll never see him again."

"We best get back to town and take care of that paperwork," said Cobb, "like he said."

"Yeah," Joiner agreed. Both men turned their horses and started back toward Rat's Nest.

"Don't worry about Slocum, Charlie," said Cobb. "He can take care of himself. If them three ain't already killed each other, he'll get them all."

"Yeah," Joiner said. "I know. It ain't that. I'm just going to miss him. That's all. I kind of got used to having the son of a bitch around, you know?"

"Yeah," Cobb said. "I like him too."

"Is he really going to be all right, Eddie?" Joiner said. "I mean with the law?"

"Don't worry about that," Cobb said. "He's riding up into old Sheriff Tom Hunter's county. Hell, I'll just send Hunter a wire right away and tell him what's happened down here. Why, when Hunter finds out that Harman had Bud killed, that's all he'll need to know. Him and Bud went back a long ways together. Hell, Hunter's likely to give old Slocum a medal or something."

"All right, well, let's get our ass on into town lickety-split and get that wire sent out," said Joiner. He kicked his horse in the sides and loped out in front of Cobb. Cobb whipped up his own mount to stay with him.

Axel had finally worked his way around to a point where he figured he must be right above and behind Harman. The blood had quit running down his neck too. It was all dried and clotted, but there was a painful throbbing on the side of his head now. He moved easily toward the road. Just there, the road ran along the side of a gently rolling hill, so if Harman was still on this side of the road, Axel would come up above him. Above and behind. He would be looking down on Harman's back. That was just fine with him. He forgot all the thoughts he'd had and the threats, he'd made about shooting kneecaps and such. His head hurt, and he was tired, thirsty, and hungry. If he could get a clean shot at Harman's back, he'd take it. Just kill the son of a bitch, take the money, and get the hell out of there as fast as he could.

Close to the top where he would be able to look out over the edge and down onto the road, Axel dropped back down on his belly. It was sore from all the crawling, and it angered him to have to assume that position again, but it seemed like the only safe thing for him to do. He inched his way cautiously toward the edge. He took the hat off his head and set it aside, then dragged himself another couple of inches. Stretching his neck, he could see the road below. He saw the black horse lying there a little farther down the road. He expected Harman to be just below him, as Harman must have worked his way up toward where Axel had been.

He couldn't see Harman, though. He inched a bit further, and then he saw him. It seemed sudden, and it startled him. Goddamn, he thought. There he is. Right there. Straight below. One well-placed shot right between the shoulder blades would do it. It wouldn't even take a rifle. A revolver shot would do as well. He was just right there. Axel congratulated himself on his calculations. He had come up in exactly the right place. All right, he told himself, now is the time. He laid the rifle down carefully, not wanting to make the smallest sound. He even worried about his breathing being too loud. He was close. He was real close.

Holding his breath, he lifted his right arm and moved it back toward the six-gun on his hip. He managed to pull it out, but reaching out with it over the edge to aim it down at Harman's back was awkward. Damn. He would have to inch up a little more. He held the six-gun out ahead of himself so that it would be ready just as soon as he got into the proper position. He scooted.

Down below, Harman sat ready with his rifle. He was watching the far side of the road where he had last seen Axel trying to work his way down closer for a good shot. Harman was tense and nervous. He knew that Axel was an expert, deadly shot with rifle or revolver. That was why he had hired the man in the first place. He told himself that he should have been more selective with his first long shot a little while ago. He should have aimed for Axel instead of Harley. Damn it, without Axel, Harley would most likely have just run for it. He had no gumption on his own. Never did. But Axel was stubborn and mean. Once he got a notion in head, it was hard turning him back away from it. Axel was the one he should have shot first.

Something sprinkled down on his back and shoulders. Dirt. He spun to the side and over on his back, at the same time raising the rifle and snapping off a shot. He saw blood splatter from the hand up above him, and a revolver fell down the side of the hill to land almost by his side.

"Yow!" yelled Axel. He flung himself backwards, rolling over and over down the back side of the hill. He finally came to a stop against a scrub oak, and he scampered quickly around behind it. It wasn't much cover, but it was all he had. Trembling with pain and anger and fear, he looked at his right hand, and where the thumb should have been, there was nothing but a short stump of raw flesh dripping blood.

"Goddamn you, Harman," he shouted. "Now you've gone and shot off my shitting-ass thumb." And then he realized that he had no gun. He had laid his rifle aside up on the rise, and he had lost his six-gun along with his thumb. "Oh, shit," he said out loud. "Oh, shit."

18

"Come on down, Axel," said Harman. "I won't kill you. Come on."

"The hell you wouldn't, you double-crossing donkey's ass," Axel said. "You've shot off my ear and my thumb already."

"I'm sorry about that, Axel," Harman said. "But you were trying to kill me. Admit it. You were fixing to shoot me in the back just now. You weren't even going to give me a chance. Were you now?"

"Well, you shot first, goddammit," Axel whined. "And you killed Harley. You never give him no chance. We was just coming out to join you. That's all."

"Sure you were, Axel," Harman said. "But, hey, that's all behind us now. All this money I got with me'll go better split twice than three times."

"It'd be even better not split at all, wouldn't it?" Axel said.

"Is your thumb really shot off, Axel?" Harman said. "Is it your right thumb?"

Axel started to answer, but he caught himself. If he let Harman know what lousy shape he was really in, he would be a goner for sure. He couldn't shoot, even if he had a gun. The rifle was just up there on the rise, but even if he

were to run and get it, he couldn't operate it. Not without
his right thumb. All Harman had to do was just crawl on
up over that little rise, walk a few feet, and blast away. It
would all be over. Just like that. He decided to try a bluff
and then run for it.

"It was my right thumb, all right, you chickenshit bastard," he said, "but I'm just as good with my left hand as
I ever was with my right. You ought to know that, and I'm
just waiting for you to poke your shitty head up over that
rise. Come on, Harman. I'll blow a fucking hole in your
head."

He stood up and started backing away quietly and easily,
watching the edge of the rise for any sign of an approach
from Harman. He shot a quick glance over his shoulder.
Some twenty yards back was a grove of scrub oak. He
backed away a little further. To keep his bluff alive, he
shouted, "Come on, you son of a bitch." Then he turned
and ran hard for the grove.

Harman waited, watching the hilltop above him. Axel had
stuck a gun hand out over it before. He might be stupid
enough to try it again. Harman didn't really think so,
though. He thought that Axel was trying to lure him into a
trap, get him to climb the rise and then shoot him as he
was struggling over the top. He tried to recall if he had ever
seen Axel shoot with his left hand, and he couldn't be sure.
He'd never paid that much attention to the gunhands. He
knew that Axel was good, though, and he knew that guns
were Axel's profession, damn near his whole life. If anyone
could shoot with a left hand, it would be Axel.

He had dropped a six-shooter when Harman had shot his
thumb, but he could easily have another, or a rifle. Harman
waited. At last, his patience almost gone, he called out,
"Axel, this is stupid. We might sit here all day like this.
Come on down. Let's talk things over." There was no answer. Slowly, Harman stood up. He kept his eyes on the
top of the hill and began walking backward up the ditch

beside the road. He stumbled over a rock and nearly fell. Regaining his balance, he continued backing away.

The hilltop on his right became lower and lower until there was no hill at all. Leaning to his right, Harman tried to peer around the hill, but it was no use. He walked out in the open field to look back to the place where Axel should be. He saw no sign of life. Holding his rifle ready, he walked toward a lone scrub oak. He judged it to be just about on line with where he had been hiding when he shot Axel's thumb. He walked slowly, his eyes darting all around. There was still no sign of Axel.

Reaching the lone tree, Harman saw blood on the ground. He stood a moment looking all around. Then he saw the rifle on the ground up by the hilltop. He walked toward it, and he almost stepped on Axel's thumb. Damn, he thought, I really did shoot the damn thing clean off. He stepped on up to the edge and looked over. Axel's six-gun was still down there where he had dropped it.

Harman couldn't be sure, but it was beginning to look to him as if Axel had pulled a bluff on him. It was beginning to look as if Axel had run for it, on foot, unarmed and with a missing ear and thumb. He grinned at the thought. If he was right, Axel was no longer a threat. He shouldn't waste any more time. There might be pursuit from Rat's Nest, and he too was on foot. He had better get going and try to make a farmhouse as quickly as possible, get a quick meal, and buy a horse. He picked up the rifle, sat down on the edge of the hill, and slid down to the ditch beside the road. There he picked up the six-gun. He walked the distance to his dead horse, jerked loose the saddlebags, and slung them over his left shoulder. Then he started walking down the road.

Slocum rode up on the bodies of two horses and one man. He didn't recognize the man, but the horses were a roan and a sorrel, just what old Gorman had said the two outlaws rode out on. He dismounted and checked the hooves. Sure enough, one had a shoe with a visible nick in it. So there were only two men left. Harman and whichever one of these two was still alive. And this man was unhorsed. He found a rifle in the scabbard on the side of one of the dead animals. He took it. The scabbard on the other horse was empty. He also took the dead man's six-gun. Then he mounted up and started riding again. He still rode easy, almost casual.

Back in Rat's Nest, Cobb sat behind the sheriff's desk while Joiner paced the floor. The gang of ranchers and cowhands still milled around in the street, and they had been joined by almost all the townspeople and some from outside of town. People stood in the street gawking at the shell of the Hi De Ho. The boldest ventured inside to look more closely at the ruins. Now and then someone shouted that he had found a piece of one of the blasted gunmen.

Thurman came riding into town, having gone back to Joiner's ranch to inform the women there that everything was settled. He'd also had the sad chore of reporting the one casualty of the big battle. Mrs. Thurman and Julia rode in Thurman's wagon, driven by one of the ranch hands. The women looked at the shell of the Hi De Ho in amazement. "Good riddance," said Mrs. Thurman. Thurman's hand Pete came walking over to join them. He took the hat off his head and nodded a greeting to each of the women. Then he looked at his boss.

"Charlie and Eddie come back," he said. "They're over in the sheriff's office. Slocum's still out there after them three that got away."

Julia ran to the sheriff's office as fast as she could go. When she broke through the door, Joiner grabbed her in his arms. She held him tight for a moment, then pulled back and looked into his eyes. "Thank God it's over," she said. "But poor Myrtle. I can't believe it, Charlie."

"I know," Joiner said. "And we haven't even had time to think about it, to grieve over her."

"And John," she said, "he's out there all by himself after three men?"

"He insisted," said Joiner. "I tried to go along with him. Eddie too. But he insisted that we come back here."

"I'm all done here," Cobb said, pushing back from his desk. "The telegram's been sent and the paperwork's all done. Now I'm riding after Slocum. Ain't nothing to keep me here."

"I'll go with you," Joiner said. He looked into Julia's eyes. "All right?"

"Go on," she said, "but be careful."

The sun was almost directly overhead, and Axel was now staggering. He was not used to long walking, and a throbbing pain shot through his body from his left ear, and another from where his right thumb should have been. His entire body felt as if it had been beaten up one side and down the other with a length of two-by-four. He was hungry, and he desperately wanted a drink of water. And to compound all his other problems, he had completely lost his sense of direction. He had begun to feel such deep self-pity that he was no longer even angry. He no longer wanted to kill Harman. He no longer thought about the money. He wanted to find a house where he could beg for a drink of water and then a bit of food. That was all. It was all, and it was everything.

Slocum had not ridden far from the site of his first stop when he saw the body of the black horse in the road ahead. So both survivors were on foot, he mused. A bunch of damn fools, he thought, to kill all the horses. He moved ahead slowly watching the sides of the road. Soon he was there beside the remains of the black horse. A shame, he thought, it had been a fine animal. He looked around from the saddle, and he saw the boot prints leading to the ditch beside the road. He dismounted and walked over there.

He could see where one man had crouched there beside

the road, probably Harman, he figured. Harman had been riding the black horse. Then he saw what looked to be dried drops of blood. He followed them up the side of the hill. The blood trail was more clear up there, and there was a thumb. A little more checking told him that one man, wounded, had run across open country on foot. He wouldn't get far, and he wouldn't move fast. He could be picked up any time. Slocum went back down to the road. A little more looking around told him that the second man, almost certainly Harman, was walking straight ahead.

Satisfied that he had learned all he could there, Slocum mounted up again and walked the Appaloosa over to the nearby stream for a drink of water. He was still in no hurry. If anything, knowing that both surviving outlaws were on foot, he was even more relaxed. He took a drink himself, and then he allowed the Appaloosa to drink its fill. Finally he mounted up again, and he moved back into the road to follow the boot prints there.

Thoughts of Myrtle kept him going. Remembrances of the way she had cared for him while he was laid up from a shot fired from ambush, the sound of her voice, the smell of her hair, the way she had looked when she was walking away in her tight jeans, the sight and the feel of her naked flesh, the way she had stood beside the men, gun in hand. All these things and more. But more than all the rest, the way she had looked as she died in his arms. They kept him going, and they kept him hard.

Harman saw the rider coming up behind him. He didn't recognize the man or the horse, a big Appaloosa. It was not another of his gunhands coming to get even with him for having run out on him. It might be someone working with Joiner. They had said that Joiner had a stranger working with him. It might just be some drifter riding by. Harman had two thoughts, though. First, he didn't want to take a chance that it might be an associate of Joiner. Second, he wanted that big horse. He turned, stood still, and raised his rifle.

Slocum saw the man he figured to be Harman raise the rifle. He cranked a shell into his own Winchester and raised it quickly to his shoulder. He aimed dead on and squeezed the trigger. The Winchester bucked and roared, and in the distance Harman jerked and fired, his own shot going wild. He tried to work the lever again, but he could not. He staggered. He fell forward on his face. Slocum rode on down.

He sat on the back of the Appaloosa looking down at the body. It was still. He knew that the man was dead. Damn fool, he said to himself. He swung down out of the saddle and picked up Harman's weapons. He dropped the six-gun into his own saddlebags along with the other he had collected, and he tied the rifle behind his saddle with the extra one he had there. Then he pulled the saddlebags off Harman's shoulder. Curious, he opened the flaps, first one, then the other. They were filled with cash. Now he knew he would have to go back to Rat's Nest one more time. He flung the saddlebags across the Appaloosa's rump. Now there would be plenty of time to ride down the other one, the one with the missing thumb, the last one. He mounted up, turned around, and started back the way he had come.

He didn't go far, though. He rode back only to the spot where he had found the thumb off the side of the road. He looked for an easy place for his Appaloosa to climb the rise, and he went off the road again. The blood trail was easy enough to follow for a while, and by then he figured that the man had to have headed for the clump of trees ahead. He rode on down there and looked around. There was no sign of the one-thumbed man. Slocum moved back out of the trees and looked around some more.

He could find no definite sign indicating which way across the grassland the man had gone. He decided to ride in a sort of circle, heading northwest for a while, then sweeping south and back southeast to the road again. He could pretty well estimate a range beyond which the wounded man on foot would not have been able to go. If the circle failed to locate the man, then he would make a smaller circle and then a smaller one until he found him. He rode easily northwest.

Axel stumbled onto the road before he knew it. Tripping over the rocks at the edge of the ditch, he fell on his face. He raised himself up and realized that he had inadvertently turned around and gone back where he had come from. He wasn't at all sure, though, just where on the road he might be. He studied the road to the north and then to the south, and he couldn't tell. He still had no idea which way to go for the nearest home, the nearest horse and meal, the nearest water.

"Looky up yonder," said Cobb, pointing ahead on the road.

"I see it," Joiner said. "Come on."

They rode ahead quickly to the site of the two dead horses and the body of Harley. "That's Harley," Cobb said. "That leaves just Axel and Harman. No way to tell whether Harman killed him or Slocum did."

"I'd say Harman," Joiner said. "Slocum wouldn't have killed the horses."

"Someone took his guns too," Cobb said. "Let's get on down the road."

They soon came up on the black horse and then a little farther along, the body of Harman himself. "Now it's just Slocum and Axel," Joiner said. "And Axel's on foot. Slocum will have him for sure."

"He's likely already got him," said Cobb.

"What do we do from here?" Joiner asked. "We don't know which way they went."

"Let's stay on the road for a bit," Cobb said.

* * *

Axel decided that the only safe thing for him to do was to stay on the road. He had already lost his way once by trying to travel off the road. He would walk north. He would have to come to something sometime. If nothing else, he should come to the stream where Harman had watered his horse. That is, unless he was already north of that spot. He didn't think so. Somehow he thought that he had wandered back south. He wasn't sure. But he'd walk north anyhow. There was nothing south of him but Rat's Nest and a gallows. He staggered ahead.

"Rider coming," said Joiner.

"Yeah," Cobb said.

They kept moving, and so did the rider from the north. Soon Cobb recognized the man. "It's Sheriff Hunter," he said. They hurried ahead to meet Hunter. Then all three riders stopped their mounts.

"Howdy, Eddie," said Hunter. "Is it Sheriff Cobb now?"

"Aw, I don't know about that," Cobb said. "I'm still a deputy. It's just that we got no sheriff right now."

"I sure hated to hear about ole Bud," Hunter said. "Have you got that Harman?"

"We found him in the road back yonder a ways," Cobb said. "Slocum must have got him. There's one outlaw left loose. The one they called Axel. We didn't see him nor Slocum anywhere along the way. You seen anyone on your way down?"

"Nary a soul," Hunter said.

"That means they're back behind us and off the road somewhere," Cobb said. "We better turn back. You want to ride along with us?"

"I don't mind," Hunter said.

Hunter reached out to shake Joiner's hand. "Glad to know you, Joiner," he said. "Say, wasn't it your ranch that was the cause of all this?"

"That's right," Joiner said.

"Glad you got it back," said Hunter.

"Thanks," said Joiner. "Well, let's go."

They rode back toward Rat's Nest, and along the way, Cobb and Joiner showed the bodies on the road to Hunter. "Once we finish up with Axel," Cobb said, "I'll send someone out with a wagon to take care of this mess."

A little further down the road, they saw Axel. He was staggering toward them, dirty, bloody, and exhausted. He was unarmed. He didn't even see to notice that three men were riding toward him. He stumbled and fell on his face, and he lay there still for a long moment. The riders looked at one another, wondering if he had just died there before their eyes. Then he moved. He struggled slowly to his feet, and he raised his head to look down the road. Then, for the first time, he saw them. "Water," he said, and his voice was at once raspy and whiny.

Cobb urged his horse forward as he loosened the canteen from the saddle. Riding up beside the wretch, he held the canteen out by its strap. Axel reached greedily for it, and then Cobb saw the mess where his right thumb should have been. He wondered who had done that. Harman probably, he thought. Slocum would have finished the job. Axel fumbled with the canteen, finally holding it under his right arm so he could unscrew the cap with his left hand. At last he tilted the canteen to his parched lips and drank desperately. Cobb reached down and pulled the canteen away from him. "That's enough," he said.

Axel whimpered, looking after the canteen. "You got any food?" he sniveled. "I'm 'bout to starve."

Hunter reached into a side of his own saddlebags and pulled out a piece of beef jerky. "Here," he said, and tossed it at Axel, who caught it by slapping it against his chest with his left hand. He fumbled to clutch it, then started gnawing at it voraciously. Hunter looked toward Cobb. "What're you going to do with him?" he asked.

"Well," said Cobb, "I don't know. I was thinking that I

wouldn't have to worry about it. I was thinking that Slocum would have killed them all by now."

"I wish John was here," said Joiner.

"Well, he ain't," Hunter said, "and you're the law here, Eddie. We can't just sit here all day. You're going to have to make a decision of some kind."

"Axel," Cobb said, raising his voice, "you're under arrest for cattle rustling and suspicion of murder and attempted murder."

"What murder?" Axel said. "What attempted murder? You ain't got nothing on me. I was hired to hang around the Hi De Ho and throw out troublemakers. That's all."

"A judge and jury will sort it all out," Cobb said. "Now turn around and start walking."

"Walking?" Axel protested. Knowing that he was in the hands of the law, Axel suddenly grew bold. "That there's cruel and unusual, ain't it? You can't do that. I'm your prisoner."

"I'd be glad to let you ride, Axel," Cobb said, "if there was another horse. There's three dead ones down the road there, and I figure you killed at least one of them. Now get going."

Axel turned slowly and started walking. His steps were labored and painful. "You'll have to get me a lawyer," he said. "I get a good lawyer and I'll go free. You know that? You ain't got no proof on me. I never rode with the rustlers. The ranch hands done the rustling. I just set there in the Hi De Ho keeping order. That was my job. And I didn't do no killing nor no attempted killings. And you can't prove it on me neither."

Joiner was riding along between Cobb and Hunter. They rode slowly behind the staggering Axel. "You know," Joiner said, "he's right. There's no way we can prove where Axel was at when any of them things took place."

"A good prosecution might get him just by proving his association with the bunch that's known to be guilty," Hunter said. "Might."

"That's mighty slim," Joiner said.

Hunter reached over and tapped Joiner on the shoulder. He gestured toward the right. Joiner looked and recognized the Appaloosa. "It's Slocum," he said. "Hold up."

They stopped their horses, and Axel stopped walking. He turned around and stood weaving as he stared at them. "What's up?" he asked.

"Axel," Cobb said, "I been thinking it over. You were right. I got nothing to hold you on. You're free to go."

"What do you mean?" Axel asked.

"Just what I said," Cobb answered. "Take off. Go wherever you want to go. I can't arrest you without no evidence."

"Mr. Hunter," Joiner said, "you've got a long ride home. Why don't you ride back to my ranch with us and have a good meal and a couple of drinks? Maybe spend the night and start home fresh in the morning."

Hunter looked off to his right again at the approaching rider. "Thanks," he said. "I'll take you up on that."

The three riders kicked their mounts into gallops and rode past Axel. He twirled, watching them, amazed. "Hey," he called out. "You can't leave me out here like this. I'm hurt. I'm on foot. Come back here. You got to help me."

Joiner turned around in his saddle and pointed off toward Slocum. "Hey, Axel," he yelled. "There's a rider coming yonder. Maybe he'll help you out."

They rode on. Axel looked off in the direction Joiner had pointed, and he saw the rider. He squinted. He wondered who it could be. Joiner and the law had already come after him, and they had let him go. Harman was dead. It couldn't be anyone after him anymore. He'd wait and ask the rider for help. He poked the last bite of the piece of jerky into his mouth and gnawed.

Slocum soon moved down onto the road. When he saw Axel, he sheathed his Winchester. It was obvious that he wouldn't need it. He saw that the man was unarmed, saw where the thumb was missing and an ear had been nicked.

It was the man he was after, all right. Axel started to speak, but something stopped him. It was the look in the rider's eyes.

"Howdy, stranger," Axel said, his voice faltering. "I could sure use a little help. I been hurt, and I lost my horse. I need a good meal."

"What do they call you?" Slocum asked.

"Axel. They call me Axel. Man, I'm hurting bad. I'm in pain here."

Slocum put his hand on the butt of his Colt. "We could put an end to that real quick," he said.

"No," Axel said. "Wait a minute. Ain't no call for that. What would you want to go killing me for?"

"You're the last one," Slocum said.

"You're riding with Joiner," Axel said. "Right?"

"That's right," Slocum said.

"Well," said Axel, "he was just here. Him and the sheriff. Two sheriffs. They let me go. They admitted they didn't have no reason to hold me. So you can let me go too. See?"

"I ain't riding with them no more," Slocum said.

"But you can't kill me in cold blood," said Axel. He held out his mangled right hand. "Look. I can't even handle a gun no more. Even if I had one. I'm unarmed, and I'm hurt. If you was to kill me, it'd be a murder. That's what it would be."

Slocum swung down off the big Appaloosa's back. He reached into his saddlebags and withdrew the blood-splattered revolver. Then he tossed it over to land between Axel's feet. "I think that's yours," he said. "I picked it up down the road yonder. I seen your thumb there. It must be your six-gun."

Axel looked down at the revolver lying there.

"I can't use it, though," he said. "I'm right-handed. See?"

He reached across his own body with his left hand and flapped the empty holster that was hanging there on his right hip. Slocum took hold of his own gunbelt with both hands, and he shifted it until the holster was hanging on his left, the butt of the Colt pointing forward. "How's that?" he said.

"No," said Axel. "No. I ain't going for it. I ain't stupid. You'll pull a cross draw on me. That's what you'll do. I ain't going for that gun."

"Whoever nicked that ear of yours did a good job," Slocum said. "I wonder if I can do as well."

"What?" Axel said.

Slocum twisted his left wrist and slowly pulled out his Colt. He took careful aim.

"What the hell're you doing?" Axel said. "You wouldn't do that."

Slocum pulled the trigger, and the roar was almost deafening, but it didn't cover Axel's shriek as the lead tore through his right ear. He clapped his hand over it, and the blood ran freely down his arm, down inside his shirtsleeve. "Goddamn," Axel said, the tone of his voice reflecting disbelief. Slocum slipped the Colt back into the holster.

"Not so good," he said. "There's still a bit of ear left dangling there. Maybe I can do better the next time."

"No, you son of a bitch," shouted Axel. He dropped to his knees and grabbed up the revolver from the dirt with his left hand. Thumbing back the hammer, he raised it to fire, but before he could pull the trigger, Slocum had performed the wrist-twisting draw again and fired. The bullet tore into Axel's chest. Axel leaned back and looked down as his fingers relaxed, and he dropped the gun. His hands both moved to the wet, sticky new hole in his chest, and he felt the hot blood pumping out in spurts. He looked up at Slocum, his eyes wide, his mouth hanging open. Then he pitched forward on his face, never to move again. Slocum holstered his Colt and shifted the belt back around where it belonged. "It's done," he said.

He rode up to the front of the ranch house, and he felt himself flooded with memories. They would have been good memories had it not all ended so abruptly and so horribly. Joiner, having heard his approach, came out on the porch. "John," he said. "Get down and come on in. I'm sure glad to see you. I didn't know if we'd ever see you again."

"You wouldn't have," Slocum said, "if it hadn't been for this." He pulled the extra saddlebags off the back of his horse and tossed them at Joiner's feet. "It's the money Harman was taking off with," he said. "I don't know how much is in there. I ain't counted it."

"Did you take some out for yourself?" Joiner asked.

"No," Slocum said. "All I done was open the flap and look to see what was in there."

"Well, come here," said Joiner. He reached into the bag and pulled out a stack of bills. Counting them quickly, he reached in for more. Slocum hadn't moved. Joiner walked over to stand beside the big Appaloosa. He held the money up for Slocum to take.

"I didn't do this job for money," Slocum said.

"But I promised to pay you when it was done," Joiner said. "Here. Take it."

Slocum took the bills and stuffed them into his shirt pocket.

"Now come on inside," Joiner said. "Sit for a spell and have a couple of drinks. Spend the night. Get a good night's rest. Maybe things'll look different in the morning."

"Sorry," Slocum said. "Things won't never look different around here to me again. I wish you all the luck in the world, Chuckie boy, and all the happiness too, you and Julia. But I just can't go back in that house. So long, pardner."

Slocum rode northwest. He didn't have a specific destination in mind. Perhaps the mountains. He wanted to be far away from south Texas. He rode along with many conflicting images swimming through his head. He saw Myrtle's face, smiling up into his own. He saw her as she walked away away from him going into the kitchen, her hips and ass tight and swinging in her jeans. He saw her leaning over him, spoon-feeding him as the gunshot wound still throbbed in his shoulder. He recalled vividly the luxury of her bodily charms, the ecstasy of her many and varied caresses.

He was lucky having known her, he told himself, however briefly. Losing her was perhaps the most painful thing that had ever happened to him. He knew that time was a healer. He knew that even this would heal. But he also knew that it would leave a terrible scar. He rode on, no longer even trying to push the painful memories out of his mind. They were too much a part of him. They would always be with him.